M.C. Schmidt

MAD
AS
BIRDS

Black Rose Writing | Texas

This is a work of fiction. Names, characters, businesses, places, events, and incidents are either the products of the author's imagination or used in a fictitious manner. Any resemblance to actual persons, living or dead, or actual events is purely coincidental.

ISBN: 978-1-68513-631-4
PUBLISHED BY BLACK ROSE WRITING
www.blackrosewriting.com

Printed in the United States of America
Suggested Retail Price (SRP) $18.95

Mad as Birds is printed in Minion Pro

*As a planet-friendly publisher, Black Rose Writing does its best to eliminate unnecessary waste to reduce paper usage and energy costs, while never compromising the reading experience. As a result, the final word count vs. page count may not meet common expectations.

MAD AS BIRDS

A stranger has come
To share my room in the house not right in the head,
A girl mad as birds

Bolting the night of the door with her arm her plume.

- Dylan Thomas

PROLOGUE

The Art Exhibition, 1947

Florence was pleased with the look of her portraits in the moon glow. She had arranged them just so around the pond, and the touch of realism from that muted light made the moon itself look counterfeit, like a paper disc pasted onto the sky. Every oil-painted mouth seemed to scream. Every masterfully rendered eye bulged. Every wound bled. She found the illusion fitting for the occasion—the real appearing unreal, the unreal coming to life.

Seven canvases hung on easels of sticks and limbs, which she'd gathered from the surrounding woods and placed so that each grotesque painting overlooked the water. The displays appeared almost human—frail bodies with faces contorted in horror. At the base of each easel, she'd piled kindling for the grand finale when she would set each of those masterpieces ablaze.

Hearing a scream in the distance, she froze and tilted her head in the direction of The Castle. More screaming followed, multiple voices yelling words she couldn't make out. Still, she knew what they were saying. They'd found Sebastian. Florence had left him propped on the settee in the common room where one of the other artists was bound to come across him sooner or later. Now, they would come looking for her. Once they found her, the art exhibition could begin.

Florence stood beneath her painting of Sebastian, the wet grass staining the cuffs of her suit pants. Face to face with his portrait, she smiled. Sebastian grimaced back at her, his eyes unblinking and terrified. "How do I look, baby?" she asked, extending her arms to show off her necktie and dress shirt, clothing that once belonged to him. In their time together, they often swapped clothes, grabbing whatever was closest at hand after a shower or a session in bed. Tonight, she had rolled her shirtsleeves to the elbows the way he wore them when he was working. He might have said she looked alluring, if he were still able.

After a moment of remembering their time together, she moved to the bonfire she'd built in the field between the pond and the woods. Carefully, she removed a burning log and held it like a torch. She could hear birds shuffling in the trees behind her, disturbed by her activity or possibly just aware of the moment's significance. She carried her torch back to Sebastian's portrait and laid it at its base. The kindling glistened with turpentine from her studio, and it caught with a satisfying whoosh. She rose and met his eyes again. "Goodbye, baby," she said. "Thank you for your sacrifice."

In the distance came the familiar groan of The Castle's giant double doors being opened. Hurried voices followed. Florence felt a fluttering in her chest. It was nearly time.

She moved to the edge of the pond, to an area she'd left free of displays, and took a seat on the ground, cross-legged. Her pants were instantly sopping from the grass. She raised her face to the sky and closed her eyes. Silently, in the way that had taken her months to perfect, she began to summon the goddess.

The other six artists were now searching the grounds for her. Their voices were close. Florence made her body into an open vessel and invited the goddess in.

First, she felt a tickle on the back of her neck. With her long, elegant fingers, the goddess stroked upward through the bristles of her hair, which Florence kept short in a gentleman's tight fade. A brief smile crossed her lips, and she bolstered herself for the pain that would follow. Each time the goddess fitted herself into Florence, she experienced the intolerable feeling of her body being cracked apart. It only lasted seconds, but it never became easier to bear. The feeling was like childbirth, she assumed, although the experience was the opposite—the pain of two becoming one, while childbirth was the other way. The goddess kneeled and pressed her chest against Florence's back, chilling her body. A second later, she pushed forward, through skin and spine. When the goddess entered her, Florence's breath escaped her throat in an involuntary moan. Her torso was thrust forward when they came together, folding her body in half. The expected pain shattered through her, then she was overtaken by the power of the divine.

"Florence!" called a voice. "What in God's name?" It was Dalí, reproaching her in his thick Spanish accent.

The goddess opened Florence's eyes. She rose from the grass and greeted them with a broad grin. They were there now in the clearing, her six lambs, come for the slaughter. "Evening, fellas," she said. "Welcome to the show." They stood across the small pond from her, their skin sallow in the moonlight. The goddess opened Florence's arms to welcome them. Each man kept his gaze fixed on her.

"Your arms, Florence," said Giacometti, a sculptor who'd been at the artist's retreat for only a month.

The goddess examined Florence's outstretched arms. They were black with blood. The skin was textured with grass and dirt and soot which had clung to her as she'd prepared the exhibition and become cemented in place when the blood dried. "Yes," she said, "Sebastian had an accident." She lowered her arms and clasped them behind her back as she moved around the perimeter of the pond.

"Florence," called Traylor, an abstract expressionist, "don't come any closer."

The goddess continued forward, altering her path only slightly to keep her distance from the men, positioning herself to block their way back to The Castle.

"My God! My God, it's you!" Nolan said to Giacometti, tugging his sleeve and gesturing toward a portrait displayed to their left. There, on the canvas, was Giacometti's unmistakable hang-dog face and puff of graying hair. His eyes were closed, and his mouth was slack. His head was tipped slightly to one side, his neck slit from one ear to the other.

"And me!" said Dalí of another portrait. "All of us!" He pointed wildly from one canvas to another. "She is a mad woman!" At his direction, the others surveyed the display, each man focused on finding his own portrait.

Traylor had just discovered his own, a masterful piece that captured him screaming at a bite wound on his neck, when the goddess thrust Florence forward onto his back and sank her teeth into his skin. Traylor screamed and bucked, trying to pitch her forward into the pond. The goddess was stronger, of course. The goddess was fangs and nails. She was divine rage. Traylor staggered and fell onto his back, landing with his full weight on top of Florence's body. The goddess pushed him off into the grass. She'd begun to rise again when the other artists rushed forward as a group and tackled her to the ground. She'd expected them to be cowards, these dandies, but they piled onto her, pinning Florence's arms and legs. So much the better if they stuck around to fight. It only meant she needn't hunt them one by one.

After throwing aside the two who held her arms, her breath was unexpectedly taken—not from the weight of the knees and shoulders on her chest, but from something inside her. *Stop!* called a voice in her mind. *Something isn't right!* It was Florence, crying out to her. The goddess squeezed Florence tighter, reminding her that after this sacrifice, they would be one—powerful and free to roam the world outside these grounds. But Florence resisted. She'd gotten cold feet. The goddess should have known.

At that moment, when she was fighting Florence's attempt to expel her, the painter, Delvaux, rushed forward with a heavy log from the pond's bank and used it to strike her on the temple. All at once, the scene went black.

•   •   •

The six artists stood over her. Traylor held a handkerchief to the bite on his neck. Nolan sounded as if he might cry when he pointed out their duty to call the authorities about Sebastian's murder. The others nodded their agreement. Each of them but Dalí. Beside him stood a seventh figure, unseen and whispering in his ear. *Did he really want to involve himself in a murder investigation? Would his reputation survive a scandal?* "No," he said. "We bury Sebastian, then we go from this place."

Several of them protested. "What about Florence?" they demanded.

The voice beside Dalí fed him the proper reply: "Florence? Leave her. She is disturbed. Without Sebastian to support her, it is only a matter of time before she finds her way to a sanitarium. She is none of our concern." He raised his hand to indicate her exhibition. "We destroy this, and we go." Traylor began again to object, but Dalí repeated more forcefully, "We destroy this, and we go!" The others were reluctant, but the goddess had the power to convince them.

They set fire to each of the portraits, then returned to The Castle to deal with Sebastian's body. The goddess observed the unconscious woman in the grass. It was a pity, human weakness. Soon enough, the artists would complete their unpleasant task and depart. Florence would awaken and scurry off too, ashamed of what she had done. Just as Dali said, it would mean the madhouse for the poor girl, a sickening waste of her talents.

As for the goddess, she would remain at The Castle, alone, trapped until a stronger host could find her.

CHAPTER 01

I.

Mr. Allison was still talking, but I'd zoned out. He was focused on Jack anyhow, talking about me rather than to me. I was staring at my knees, thinking about the time I'd gotten Student of the Month in fifth grade, which was the only other time I'd been in a principal's office. There wouldn't be any handshakes or Pizza Hut coupons this time, though. All I was going to get out of this mess was a boot up my ass.

Out of nowhere, Jack rapped me on the thigh with his knuckles. He gestured not to slouch in my chair, and I sat straight up like Mr. Eager-to-Please. They were both staring at me—Mr. Allison from across his desk and Jack from the chair beside mine. Their expressions said I had a lot of nerve trying to sit comfortably at a time like this. I wasn't comfortable at all, of course. Still, what did my posture matter? Posture wouldn't change anything. "Sorry," I said. They didn't respond, just used their silence to hold me frozen like that before going back to discussing me.

You'd think all my years of being a model student would be a consideration here. Context or whatever. But popular opinion said I was a monster—the kids at school thought so, and my teachers and people online. The TV news anchors even scowled when they reported about me, or about the "unnamed classmate," which was what they called me because I was a minor.

My eyes wandered to the window behind Mr. Allison's desk. It was May and still spring, but the sky was summer blue. I noticed the speck of a far-off airplane and clamped my eyes shut at a flash image of it crashing. This was something my brain had done for as long as I could remember—see a plane, imagine it crashing. I wasn't wishing for it to happen. I didn't want the passengers to die or anything. I just couldn't help picturing the fire and the smoke and the crazy whirligig of its wings as it spun bigger and bigger, falling to earth. I always assumed everyone had crazy thoughts like this. But as I lowered my eyes from Mr. Allison's window, I wondered if I'd been wrong, if I should have recognized it as a warning sign that I was a psycho. If I'd told someone about the planes, would they have gotten me help? Would I still be sitting with Jack in the principal's office?

Mr. Allison got my attention by saying my name, "Milo," followed shortly with the word, "expelled." I'd known it was coming, but my face still went hot when he said it out loud. I felt like a baby how quickly I turned to Jack, pathetically looking to big brother to save me.

"You can't expel him. It's almost summer break," Jack said. "The school year's basically over."

"He'll be given zeros for his finals, but he'll maintain a passing GPA. For his senior year, however, you'll need to register him in a neighboring district."

"No, that's too extreme."

Mr. Allison pulled his face into the kind of smile that's meant to soften bad news. "I'm sorry, Mr. Selby, but we have no choice. The school administration has discussed the matter at length, and we feel Milo's actions warrant the severest punishment."

If he'd been looking at me when he said it, that I deserved the severest punishment, I probably would have started bawling. It would have made it too overwhelming, the feeling of being scolded and trapped. He'd gone back to ignoring me, though. He just sat there and sentenced me without even turning to face me.

Jack leaned forward and propped his elbows on the desk. "Mr. Allison, you know what he's been through this year. It's been terrible for both of us, but Milo's only seventeen. He wasn't *even* seventeen at the time. Mom and Dad died when he wasn't even seventeen."

"Mr. Selby—"

"No. I'm not saying he didn't make a mistake. He was stupid, obviously. But you've got to see how the trauma of losing our parents clouded his judgement." He sat back and put a hand just above my knee like an act of wholesome brotherly love. My ass was on the line, so I didn't pull away from him. Still, it's uncool to grab a person by their leg in just about every context.

"Mr. Selby, a student died."

I felt Jack's hand tighten. "I understand, and it's tragic. But it wasn't Milo's fault."

"The district has a clear policy against bullying. Zero tolerance."

Jack's voice rose to an unattractive squall. "Bullying? Does this kid look like a bully?" He gave me a once-over and laughed, which was condescending.

"I imagine he did to Rebecca Steiner the night she died."

"God," I muttered without meaning to.

"Excuse me?" Jack asked. He whipped his head toward me. His eyebrows were up. His eyes looked crazy. Mr. Allison was looking at me now, too.

"I just want to go home," I said. "This isn't doing any good. And what does it even matter if they send me to a new school? Everyone here hates me now, anyway."

"Ms. Steiner was one of our most popular students," Mr. Allison said, as if he was explaining why their hate was justified.

I pinched the fabric of my T-shirt collar into my eyes. It was comforting, like a hole I could hide in, so I buried my face in that darkness, breathing warm air onto my chest and stomach. I listened to Mr. Allison tell Jack about a contact list they'd printed for neighboring school districts and registration deadlines so I could start senior year on time. Jack didn't say much more. After a few minutes, his hand wrenched my arm, and he pulled me to my feet by my armpit. The sudden brightness of the office was as blinding as a stage light.

"Come on," he said, storming past me. "Stop screwing around."

I followed him through the school, all the way to the parking lot. He was fidgeting with the key fob for his Hyundai, smashing his thumb into a button that refused to unlock the doors, when I said, "So, that sucked." I didn't mean to minimize it. Nerves made me say it.

Jack was on the other side of the car, but I still jumped when he started stabbing his keys in my direction. "I cannot even believe you, Milo! I can't believe you got yourself kicked out of school! So, what now? I have to find a job that's cool with me leaving whenever to chauffer you from some school that's God-knows-where? No big deal to you, though, right?" Literal spit hung from his lower lip.

"It's a very big deal to me," I said. That I had to clarify this to my own brother caused the tears I'd jammed up to pour out of me. I turned away so he wouldn't see.

Some drama followed—Jack beating his palm against the driver's window, Jack cursing, Jack's sanity obviously depending on the level of battery life in that key fob, both of our futures being positively affected when we finally heard the door locks turn.

We sat in the car, not talking. I pulled myself together. Jack cooled down. After a few minutes, he looked at me, breathing deeply, like he was calming himself to apologize. And he really did sound composed when he finally said, "You should be so grateful Mom and Dad are dead. It would break their hearts to see what a disappointment you've become."

II.

It was afternoon, and I was lying in bed. I was fully clothed like it was a regular school day, which, I guess, it technically was. Wednesday, I think. My phone pinged. I snaked it out of my pocket and lit the screen.

Murderer!!!! the text message read. I didn't know the number.

MAY THE GOOD LORD BLESS YOU AND KEEP YOU! I wrote back before blocking them. Whatever.

I went back to my new hobby of staring at the ceiling. I could hear Jack smashing around the kitchen, the same one Mom used to float through even after she'd put in a full workday. Jack could make the pans clang like they were crying out from abuse.

He'd grounded me after I got shit-canned from school. As my guardian, he had the legal authority to do that now. It didn't matter. It's not like it was keeping me from any plans. The only thing was, my room was mostly oil paints and canvases and the A/V equipment I'd used for my now-defunct YouTube art channel, and anything to do with art made me think of Rebecca Steiner. I had a roomful of reminders that my life had gone to hell. Lying there, I tried to do a thing that was like twisting my situation into something positive. An affirmation, I guess. It was like this—in less than a year my life had gone completely off the rails, so it stood to reason that in only a year from now I could be killing it again. Not that I'd ever actually been killing it. That was just part of the positive thinking.

I was doing that, being an optimist, when my phone pinged again. It was still in my hand, and its vibration made me think of a low-watt electric chair, like I'd been sentenced to death by the buzzing of a thousand shitty texts. I hesitated before looking. These troll messages had begun to taper off in the weeks since Rebecca died. Some days lately, I didn't get any at all.

I lit the phone screen and was surprised to see a name I recognized. Aaron Baer. Not counting elementary school when everyone liked everyone, I'd only ever had a casual friend group, but Aaron was usually a part of it. They'd all abandoned me when I became toxic, but I couldn't blame them. This was high school, survival of the fittest. I probably would have done the same to them.

U moving?? his text read.

He'd seen the For Sale sign in our yard. Jack had decided it was necessary. He said we couldn't survive the scandal if we stayed in Muncie because all of Muncie was against me. So, where would we move to escape that hate? He didn't know. He was working on it. He'd filled out some applications or put out feelers at different places. He was waiting to hear back. It seemed like overkill to me, but who was I? Just some loser, sweating over how to answer a stupid text message. It had been so long since anyone reached out to me that I was just holding the phone, staring at Aaron's message, reading it over and over. *guess so*, I sent back after thinking way too hard about it.

His response was immediate: *cool.*

Sucks… I waited a full minute for a reply, then another minute. My heart was pounding like some lovesick jerk texting his crush. Finally, I just came out and asked, *u wanna hangout?* It didn't matter that I was grounded and couldn't hang out. I just needed to know someone in my life hadn't completely written me off.

Aaron answered with the thinking face emoji, then followed it with the message, *I'm good, bro.*

It was pure reflex when I threw the phone, like a necessary release of pressure that would have otherwise caused a dangerous explosion inside me. And it worked. Once I'd flung it from my hand, I didn't feel angry at all. I wasn't mad at Aaron. I wasn't mad about the rip the phone made in the half-finished canvas I'd abandoned on my easel. I wasn't mad the phone screen cracked into an elaborate spiderweb when it struck the hardwood floor. I was okay with all of it.

"Milo!" Jack shouted.

"What?"

"Get in here!"

I rolled my eyes and slid off the bed to go see what he wanted. He was still in the kitchen, watching the aggressive boil of boxed mac and cheese noodles. "Hey," I said to him. I hung back in the kitchen doorway, keeping my distance.

"What are you doing in there?"

"Nothing."

"Nothing, huh? From out here, it sounded like you were breaking your shit."

Despite Jack's blowup in the school parking lot, he tended to keep his temper in check. He often gave off a kind of caged animal energy, though, a vibe that suggested he was keeping his cool but only with some effort. An eruption was possible. I stayed cautious because I was still learning the ropes with him. He was six years older than me, so we'd never been close as kids. When he got to high school, he was home less and less, then college took him away completely. So, what did the grown man battering around our kitchen have in common with the thirteen-year-old version of himself I remembered? Nothing more than I had in common with the eight-year-old I was at the time.

And about college, he loved to hold it over my head that he'd been forced to drop out and move home to look after me. This was bullshit. He finished undergrad two winters ago. What he'd left was the bartending job he was using to put off grad school. Dad used to complain about it constantly—how Jack was using grad school as an excuse not to grow up and get a real job at the same time he was using his bartending schedule as an excuse not to start grad school. A loser's dilemma, Dad called it. It bugged me. Mostly because I knew his anger about coming home was real; it just wasn't about school. I could see how I might not be as important as finishing a degree he'd been working toward for years. It was harder to understand how I was less important than some job pouring drinks and chatting up middle-aged mothers on their nights out.

"So, listen," he said, staring down at the stovetop, "you need to start thinking about what you want to take with you in the move. We need to downsize. You may as well get started."

"Are we moving to an apartment?" I had never lived in an apartment. I'd never lived anywhere but home.

He kept his eyes on the pot of noodles, but I saw the muscles of his jaw working before he spoke. "We have some options. I don't know for sure. Regardless, we'll have less space."

"What options?" I wasn't challenging him. I was genuinely curious. I tried to make this clear by doing my best to sound earnest.

Jack lifted the pot off the stove and moved it to the sink. He poured the hot water and pasta into a colander, steam rolling over his face like he was some pissed-off cartoon character. "Well, Milo," he said, "I guess we have a couple of options." He turned to look at me. His face was unreadable, coldly neutral. "Option one is we stay here and be pariahs. They still call me for quotes, you know? The newspaper, TV reporters. People I haven't heard from since high school text to ask me what went wrong with you. I don't know if option one appeals to you, brother, but I'm going to go ahead and override your vote just in case and say that's not going to happen."

He returned his attention to the sink, dumping the drained noodles back into the pot, then slamming it down onto the glass stovetop. "Option two is we pack up and get out of here. You pick. But remember, I already overrode your vote for staying. So, which will it be?" He tore the packet of cheese dust and dumped it over the noodles.

"No, I meant…" I began, but stopped when he slid his eyes my way. I took a beat to consider how to say it inoffensively. "I thought you meant you had an idea about where we'd go. Specifically, I mean."

His smile looked deadly. "I used to have an idea about where I'd go. Grad school, that's where I thought I'd go. But life doesn't care about our plans, does it?"

I could have called him on it, but I didn't. "I'm sorry," I said instead.

He didn't speak right away, just stared down at the stovetop, nodding to himself. He'd forgotten to turn off the burner, and the pot began to smoke. He pushed it to the back of the stove, away from the heat, then snapped off the burner's dial. An acrid smell filled the air between us.

Finally, he said, "I know you're sorry, Milo." His tone sounded a degree less harsh. "I've been thinking we need to get off the map." He glanced at me, and I nodded, trying to show him I appreciated wherever this thought had taken him. And who knew? Maybe he was right that we should disappear. Maybe the part of me that didn't want to leave home was just scared to leave Mom and Dad behind. Maybe I needed to accept that I no longer had a mom and dad to leave. "So," he continued, "my first thought was to move across the country. Leave Muncie behind. Turns out, though, I may have a solution that lets us stay in Indiana."

"I don't understand."

"That's because I haven't explained it to you yet. See, my buddy Raj, from school—we were in the same business program—he told me about some new Luddite community near South Bend. South Bend is Raj's hometown."

"Wait—Luddite? What's that again?"

"Like anti-tech. No phones or computers or whatever. Perfect for our situation, right, since you're being savaged online? If we relocated there, I could go into business with Raj. He wants to open a freight brokerage in South Bend. Says we'll make a killing."

I had no idea what a freight brokerage was, but Jack's business opportunities didn't interest me in the slightest. The anti-tech community was another story. "So, is it, like…what, an Amish town or something?"

"Nah, more like a commune—some old building they renovated and turned into a planned community. But, I mean, it's not like a cult. You come and go as you please, but everyone lives together and, I don't know, eats together and plays checkers or whatever, instead of scrolling on their phones. I don't have that exactly right, but it's something along those lines. I'm not entirely sure."

I nodded. "Cool."

"We have some money from Mom and Dad I could use as capital to start the business. I mean, it's not grad school, but it beats working for the man. We'd be the bosses, me and Raj. As for the commune, I talked to the owner this morning. I think he was sympathetic to your situation. And he liked that you were into painting, even though I told him you didn't do it anymore. He said we can take a tour whenever we want to drive up." When I didn't respond, he asked, "You have a better idea? If so, I'm all ears."

I stared past him into the kitchen of the only house I'd ever lived in. I shook my head. I didn't have any ideas at all.

"Me either," Jack said. "So, are we going to eat this mac and cheese, or what?"

I shrugged and started into the kitchen. Unexpectedly, he stopped me by pressing the tips of his fingers into my chest. I froze. I was too close to him. He was too close to me.

"Before you eat, tell me what you broke in your bedroom."

"My phone," I said, like his sour breath in my face was a truth serum.

He held us like that. *He's going to reach into my chest,* I thought. *He's going to squeeze the life out of my heart.* Slowly, his blank expression grew into what looked to be a genuine smile. "Well, that's no great loss," he said. "If everything works out, you won't need it, anyway. Not in South Bend." He reached up and smacked me on the cheek, then he turned and grabbed a fork and bowl and helped himself to a large portion of what would pass for our lunch.

III.

That night, I waited until long after he'd gone to bed, then I sneaked into Dad's office. The MacBook I'd used for homework was school property and it was still in my locker, along with some personal belongings I'd never see again, and my phone was good and truly dead. For a screen with Internet access, that only left me with Dad's PC.

I crept down the hall and eased the office door closed before turning on the light. I wasn't forbidden from the office as far as I knew; Jack had never said anything about it one way or the other. I just decided to be quiet about it because why poke the bear?

Scanning the office, I half expected to feel something significant—overwhelming emotion caused by Dad's lingering smell, or a flood of memories of happier times, or something—but no. It was just a room, empty like all the others in our house.

The PC took forever to boot. Jack hadn't given me much to work with, so it was trial and error locating the place he was thinking of moving us. Once I found it, though, holy shit.

According to a story on the *South Bend Tribune* website, the century-old building had been in disrepair for decades. A young family bought it and renovated it and were now opening it as an intentional community. Those kinds of communities had become trendy, apparently, as social media increasingly replaced face-to-face interactions, and people began to feel isolated in the real world. To me, it didn't sound so different from a regular apartment complex, other than their communal meals and ban on devices. "Strengthening the social ties of the community," they called it. Close as a clan of cavemen. It seemed a little hippy-dippy to me.

Judging from the pictures, it was an impressive gothic-looking stone mansion. More impressively, it was built back in 1890 by a guy named Stanford Kayo, who, as it turned out, was the creator of Kayo Corn Nibs. Corn Nibs was one of the most famous breakfast cereals in the world. We're talking Kleenex or Jell-O levels of universal recognizability.

I learned that Stanford Kayo came from money, one of those too-big-to-fail types. He was a trained theologian who renounced his Catholic upbringing in favor of his own kooky religious theories. These theories were what led him to found Kayo Foods. Apparently, he started out making wafers and oatmeal and, in Kayo's words, other "spiritually wholesome foodstuff." He published books and gave lectures and built the South Bend mansion as a wellness center for the elite—oil tycoons and old Hollywood and steel barons—to promote his ideas about spiritual health. The craziest thing, though, was his view on sex. In a nutshell, Kayo didn't believe any devout person should give in to sexual temptation. So, no sex ever. Not even after marriage. Not even to produce children. If I understood it right, he thought sexual climaxes were your soul's energy escaping your body. And every person only has so much soul energy before they're hollow and hell bound. He believed wholesome foods could help keep a person from sinning, so he developed a soda cracker, which he promoted as "an aid to tamp down private urges." The crackers were a hit—not because they solved masturbation, presumably, but because they were salty and delicious—

so he expanded his brand to include corn cereal meant to "dampen the sexual appetite." That product was the still-famous Corn Nibs. After his death, Kayo Foods dropped his spiritual nonsense and carried on as a regular food company. I'd been eating his masturbation crackers and abstinence nibs since I was a baby. Most people had. They just didn't know the backstory.

The hospital shut down and sat empty for decades. In the 1930s, it was bought by a rich art dealer who reopened it as an artist's retreat, which he called The Castle. I found references to a few well-known artists who'd stayed there, but I found an actual photo of Salvador Dalí posing in front of the building, staring at the camera in all his wide-eyed, mustachioed glory. I wasn't a Dalí freak personally. I thought his paintings were kind of lame. My real interest was in artists like Frida Kahlo and Caravaggio and Yayoi Kusama and too many others to name. Still, he was one of the most famous artists of the twentieth century, and the art nerd in me was star-struck.

That's about where I stopped reading. The clock on Dad's PC showed two-thirty in the morning. I went to bed, cautioning myself not to get too excited. If the past year had taught me anything, it was that life could be cruel, and it was best to keep your expectations low.

<h1 style="text-align:center">IV.</h1>

Jack set up a tour for the Friday of that week. We left early, and I spent most of the two-hour drive pretending to sleep. I anticipated a punch on the arm that meant, *If I have to be awake for this, so do you.* It never came, though. He likely felt as relieved to avoid conversation with me as I was with him. Eventually, I legitimately nodded off and was startled awake when his voice thundered, "Bro, we're here." We were parked in the bend of the horseshoe shaped driveway, feet from the building's entrance.

Looking through the car window, my first impression was that we'd arrived in some land of giants. The mansion's yellow-gray brick extended as far as my view allowed. There were columns framing the double doors ahead of me. Doric columns, I knew, because I knew about art. They were thicker than I could have wrapped my arms around. Past Jack, through the driver's window, I saw the base of a large statue—a bronze woman with pleated robes and sandaled feet. From the Hyundai, I couldn't see much of her, but I recognized the statue from photos of the property I'd found online. In those photos, she'd been too blurry to really see her. "That's a big bitch," Jack said, tacky. He got out of the car for a better look. I got out too.

Déjà vu isn't the right way to explain what I was feeling, but it was something like that. Not the sense that I'd been there before as much as a feeling like I'd finally arrived somewhere I had always wanted to be. Which was nonsense, of course, since I'd only learned about it two days earlier. Looking up at the building's floors of stone and glass, I felt as insignificant as an ant. I loved that feeling. It might sound crazy, but after months of fearing I might burst from guilt and sadness, it was comforting to stand in The Castle's giant shadow and feel shrunken to something tiny and meaningless. To Jack's credit, this was exactly his point in bringing me there.

I came up beside him at the base of the statue. "Imogen Kayo," he said, reading from a plaque at her feet, "my beloved wife, who died young." He looked at me with his eyebrows raised. We would be among strangers today, and he was already practicing the persona of a good guy. "What do you think killed her?" he asked.

I shrugged. "Bears?" I knew from my research she'd died of tuberculosis.

"Yeah," he said mockingly, "probably one of those infamous South Bend Indiana bear attacks. Come on, dumbbell, let's go inside." I raised my eyes for a final look at Imogen then followed behind him.

The Castle's broad double doors opened into an entryway that was enormous and high-ceilinged. I found the echo to be disorienting. Sound seemed liquid—lilting and different from the dull tones of the real world. To our right, a curved staircase led to a second floor so high above my head I couldn't even glimpse it past the polished wood railing.

No one came to greet us, and there was no manager's office or front desk with a bell to call someone. Jack seemed as perplexed as me. When he caught me looking at him, his expression went stern like he was a man in control. He stepped forward on the worn carpet and called, "Hello?" The question returned to us on all sides.

"Just a moment!" a watery voice called. Jack seemed to hear it from his left and looked in that direction. I looked behind us, because that's where I'd heard it come from. We were both wrong. "Welcome, Mr. Selby," the voice boomed again. "I see you've brought along Milo." A second later, I heard the stuttering squeak of shoes on stairs.

"Dude," I said to Jack, pointing to direct him.

"Yes," the man on the staircase laughed, "I'm up here. So sorry. The way this entrance echoes, I feel like the Wizard of Oz delivering his screed. And I guess I am a little like the Wizard, because when you look behind the curtain, it's just little old me." He hopped off the bottom step then smiled and opened his arms as if inviting us to look over little old him.

I don't know exactly what kind of person I expected would own a historic gothic mansion, but this guy wasn't him. He was on the short side, with a beard and wild, curly, graying hair. He was wearing jeans and a short-sleeved shirt which had Northern Indiana Intentional Community silkscreened on the right breast. He had on a pair of neon running shoes, but his pudgy belly didn't give the impression he was a runner.

"You're Mr. Fishback?" Jack asked.

"At your service. But I only answer to Fish."

While he and Jack talked, I noticed the man had a sort of magician vibe about him. His movements were elegant and at odds with his scruffy look, like the life force inside him believed it was piloting a more graceful body than the grungy, squat one he really possessed.

I couldn't imagine Jack calling a grown man "Fish," so I was surprised when he grinned broadly and said, "Well, Fish, we have a long drive back. What do you say we get this tour going?"

V.

"We want each resident to be a proper fit for the community. That's our concern above all else. So, we'll take it slow, find the right people. We want to fill five to seven units to start, ten at the most. Then, we'll continue to grow at whatever pace makes sense for us as a collective."

I was hanging back a few paces behind Fish and Jack, observing the cracks of the ancient tennis courts we were walking over. The "we" he was referring to were himself, his husband, and their twin daughters. When he first mentioned his husband, I wondered if that guy had a nickname to match Fish's. Something like Chips, I thought, picturing their hilarious *Fish & Chips* embroidered bath towels. It was a huge anticlimax when he finally named his husband as Brandon.

"Hang on," Jack said, "you've got all this residential space, and you're not going to fill it up?"

"For the time being. As I said, we're taking it slow, finding the right people. Maybe you and Milo will be amongst them."

"Man…you two must be loaded if you can afford to run this place empty."

Fish stopped suddenly and raised a hand toward Jack. For a second, I thought he was going to hit him for being rude. His hand continued to rise, though, until he was pointing into the sky. I stopped and so did Jack, our eyes following his outstretched finger.

A few hundred feet from where we stood, the property was lined with a dense patch of trees. I didn't see what he was showing us at first, but then my eyes fixed on movement at the tree line—an enormous bird rising on long, pterodactyl wings, gaining speed as it ascended. "What is that?" I asked.

Fish didn't answer immediately. He stared after the bird until it was only a pinprick in the sky. "That was a great blue heron. They frequent our pond beyond those trees." He shifted his gaze to me and smiled. "Absolutely beautiful, wasn't it?" He looked at Jack who shrugged like, *whatever, man.* When they started walking again, Fish said, "Sorry,

Jack, where were we? I believe you were asking personal questions about my finances?" Jack stammered, but Fish chuckled to let him know he was kidding. "It's fine. Not to get too far into our private affairs, but we own this property outright—The Castle, the grounds, even the pond which our lovely herons call home. So, we have the luxury to build slow and smart. I have to say, though, when we posted our ad, we braced ourselves for hundreds of applications, thousands even. I had a recurring nightmare of so many applications arriving that I was literally drowning in them. But the response has been meager. Apparently, the idea of limited technology and communal living with fellow human beings was a non-starter for many people." He tossed his hand to show he wasn't bothered. "So much the better. It only proves technology is a drug, that our community is necessary."

They walked on, but I stayed where I was, thinking the great blue heron might circle back. I'd never gotten such a close look at a bird that big. Pretty soon, though, I started to feel dumb staring into the empty sky, then I had a familiar flash image of a plane smoking and falling, and I winced and looked away. Jack and Fish were far ahead and hadn't noticed I was missing, so I decided to jog to the tree line to check out the pond. The trees were a good distance away. An acre? Half a football field? I wasn't sure. I didn't farm or play sports. At any rate, it was only a minute or two before I was navigating through those trees.

The pond was small, the water calm and gently rippling. I stood for a while at the edge of it, hypnotized. I guess I got attuned to the place, because I noticed the subtlest movement across the pond from where I was standing. Raising my eyes, I saw it was another great blue heron, standing in the tall grass, studying me. As soon as I noticed it, it hopped into the trees where I couldn't see it. Curious, I walked around the pond to the opening where it disappeared, and I followed it in. Under the canopy, daylight softened to the dimness of early evening. The ground was littered with green seed pods the size of baseballs, which had fallen from the branches. I stood as still as possible, scanning around me. Taking a few steps farther in, I heard a tiny rustling to my right. I turned my head, slow and easy, and spotted the heron's narrow dinosaur head, peeking from behind a nearby tree trunk, watching me in profile with one yellow eye. Its head came to the height of my belly, tall as hell. "Whoa," I said, at which point it bounded around the tree toward me, flapping and squawking. I should have turned and run back to the clearing, but the fastest way out of its path was forward and to the left, so that's the direction I headed, deeper into the woods. It snapped at the back of my shirt, and I made some impromptu feral sound, trying to scare it away. Brush and branches scratched up my arms as I ran. I nearly tripped more than once—then I finally did and fell on my ass. I skittered backward, crab-walking a foot or two, until I cracked the back of my head against a vine-covered wall tucked into the trees. I must have hit it pretty good because my vision went blurry for a couple of seconds. I didn't register the pain. My brain had flipped over to survival mode. I leaned back against the wall and raised my leg to kick at the heron. As soon as I was in that position, though, I realized it was gone. No giant, prehistoric-looking bird. Just me, alone in the woods. I supposed I was so eager to get out of its way, I didn't notice when it stopped chasing me.

I smiled at the treetops, relieved. Turning my head, I noticed the wall I was leaning against was made of stone masonry. Stones of all different sizes were mortared together, like they'd been found and gathered rather than bought. The wall wasn't freestanding either, as I'd assumed. It was the back of a building. I didn't understand why it was hidden in the woods like that, but, of course, I didn't know shit about running an estate. Maybe it was a utility building or a hunting lodge or something to do with maintaining the pond. Was that something people did? Maintain ponds?

I got to my feet and walked the perimeter of the building. It was basically a square—maybe eight feet high and eight feet on every side. The building's door was metal, rusted the bright orange of a pumpkin. Dozens of people—kids probably, sneaking into the woods to party or have sex—had scratched their names and initials into the rust. They overlapped with one another and were fading away. Only one of the names looked new.

"Milo!" It was Jack's voice echoing through the air from somewhere far away. I'd been gone longer than I'd meant to be. He'd be pissed, but he was always pissed, so what did it matter? Still, I hightailed it out of those woods and around the pond and back through the second tree line into the open field where I'd broken off from the tour. He and Fish were nowhere to be seen, so I started jogging. When I finally spotted them, they were back at the car, staring up at Imogene Kayo's bronze statue. They were both facing me, and it felt like an eternity of them watching me before I caught up to them. "You get lost?" Jack asked. He smiled big like the friendliest fox.

I nodded, out of breath from the jog. I wasn't what you'd call physically exceptional, and my side hurt like some sharp-toothed thing had bitten into it.

"Well, I hope you liked what you saw," Fish said. "You'll be seeing a lot more of it."

I looked from Fish to Jack. Jack nodded. "Yeah, you heard the man," he said. "Pack your bags, bro."

VI.

That night in Muncie, I dreamt I was someone else.

I was in the living room of an unfamiliar house. The lights were dim, and the curtains were drawn. A hospital bed was wedged awkwardly into the room between the couch and television. I stared down at a woman in the bed. She was tiny—skinny and frail. In the dream, I was sad she was dying. In the dream, she was my mother. I'd never seen her in my life.

The room had a sick animal smell. Outside, sparrows chittered. Their voices made the woman's eyes smile. She met my gaze and blinked that smile at me. I leaned down, knowing she wanted to speak to me. In the dream, we had that kind of bond. When my ear was close to her cracked lips, she whispered that I was her very lovely girl.

Before I could answer her, I was startled by the sound of a rock hitting the picture window beyond the bed. Another rock hit, followed by another and another. The sound kept coming, ringing through the room. I looked at the woman to ask what was happening, but she only closed her eyes and left me to wonder. Carefully, I moved to the window. Sliding between the hospital bed and the television stand, my pant leg rubbed against the woman's foot, pulling off her sock. Her toes were curled and blue, with overgrown nails. She didn't move. She didn't seem to notice. I hesitated at the curtains before flinging them open. When I did, the picture window was a collage of blood and feathers. The bodies of a dozen sparrows lay broken on the brick patio. More of them were flying at the window, a platoon of birds torpedoing toward me, but I was able to close the curtains again before they struck the glass. I turned back to the woman, but she was gone. All that remained were ruts in the carpet from the hospital bed's castors and that single empty sock. When I woke up, I was crying. I cried for a good long time.

CHAPTER: 02

I.

Passing me on the grand staircase, Jack asked, "You all right there? Remember where you're going?" I was fully loaded, going up. He was empty-handed, coming down. The suitcase in my right hand was taking turns beating into my thigh and smacking against the stair rail.

"I'm fine." To prove it, I clenched my jaw and moved up the stairs two at a time. I had a case in each hand and a trash bag full of sneakers under my arm. The load was awkward, and by the time I got to the top, my lungs burned like the air on the second floor was made from something other than oxygen. That was the state I was in, huffing and sweating and buttressing myself against the second-floor railing, when an auburn-haired girl around my age appeared from the direction of our new apartment.

"Whoa," she said, stopping in her tracks and giving me a horrified look. "Do you need help? You're purple."

I want to be clear that this isn't a love story. I thought she was pretty, though, which can mess with your brain chemistry if you happen to be the type of person whose interests include pretty girls. What I'm getting at is that, for approximately the next sixty to ninety seconds, I acted like something of a douche. "No," I grunted. "I'm cool."

She shifted her weight and cocked her head, making a show of looking me over. "Oh, you're cool? Cool. So, you're just, what? Leaning on the railing, examining the carved wood? There are rabbits carved into the newel. They're cute. You should check them out."

"Mm-hmm," I said. It was about the only thing I could say while I struggled for breath.

She squinted at me. "All right. But can I take one of those suitcases from you? As a favor to me, I mean. Dad's writing, so he kicked me out of the apartment. I'm totally bored." I shook my head no. The pity on the girl's face absolutely killed me. She looked at me like I was a puppy that had tied itself up on its own lead. "Okay, well, I'm still just going to take this from you." She slipped her hand over mine in one of the suitcase's handles and tugged it out of my grip. "Ooh, this is a nice case," she said, trying to distract me. "Is it waterproof?"

She was miles down the hall with it before I had the breath to call, "It's okay. I can take it."

She stopped, then turned to face me. "Oh, my God, I'm sorry—are you a masculine hero? I didn't realize. That's lucky for me because I'm in distress—I'm only a girl, after all. Before you arrived, I was so bored I was thinking of going out hunting for drugs, or maybe a human trafficking situation I could ensnare myself in. So, by letting me carry this suitcase for you, it's possible you saved my life just now. I thank you, masculine hero. *I* thank you, and every member of my sex thanks you." She curtsied awkwardly with the heavy case and extended her free hand like she wanted me to kiss it. I was burning with embarrassment. Still, I couldn't help but notice the stains of yellow oil paint on her fingers.

By that point, I'd just about caught my breath. "I think I'm being dumb."

"You are most certainly being dumb." The girl flipped her hair and resumed walking ahead of me. "Where are we headed, Hero?"

I readjusted my remaining suitcase and garbage bag then hurried to catch up to her. "Um, two-eleven. I haven't seen it yet; I'm not sure which one it is." She didn't answer, just kept walking. "Thank you. For your help, I mean. I think you're the real hero here, probably. *My* hero," I added lamely.

I was relieved when she let it slide. "I've been at The Castle for over a week," she said. "Dad and I were the first ones to move in. Except for Fish and Brandon and the twins, obviously. So, I'm used to servitude. I've helped paint apartment walls, I've chopped vegetables for dinner, I even installed a new toilet yesterday—which, if I'm being honest, was way more fun than it sounds."

"Nobody told me there's mandatory labor involved with living here." I was trying to sound lighthearted, but I think she took me seriously.

"Oh, it's not mandatory. I wanted to. Anyway, it's in the spirit of the community." Her tone was mocking, like she wasn't totally sold on the idea of communal living either. "This suitcase is heavy." She swung it in front of her and took the handle in both hands. "What is it, like, sports trophies or something?"

I couldn't help but laugh at this. It wasn't often I was mistaken for a sports guy. I'm not sure it had ever happened before. "No, I don't do sports. It's art supplies, mostly. Paints and charcoal and colored pencils. Oh, and that case might also have some of my old Ninja Turtles. Like, thirty or so."

"That's cool. The art supplies, not the turtles. Oil or acrylic?"

As I mentioned earlier, art had become a tricky subject for me because it was so wrapped up in my head with the tragedy that brought us there. Still, what were the odds of two underage painters living in the same tiny community? I was bursting to talk to her about it, to tell her art had been my whole life since I was a little kid. It felt a little gross, but I plowed ahead, playing like the subject didn't make me think of death and loss and forced exile from the only home I'd ever known. "Acrylic?" I made a face like she'd asked if I enjoyed painting with mud. "No. Acrylic is for elementary school kids and drunk people on those *Paint and Sip* nights out. I use oils."

The girl stopped in front of an apartment door and set down my suitcase. I did the same, and she gave me a long, curious look. "What?" I asked.

"I paint too. That's weird, right?"

It was. In my whole life, I had never known anyone my age who painted outside of art class, and I told her so.

"Well, anyway…this is your apartment. You guys are right beside me and Dad. I'm Sam, by the way."

"Milo."

"Can I ask you a question, Milo?"

I nodded.

She looked me dead in the eye for a few seconds, properly staring into me. It was an unexpected shift in her demeanor, and it creeped me out a little. "When you went on your tour, did Fish tell you this place was haunted?"

I snorted, feeling foolish to have taken the bait. "Yeah, haunted by the ghosts of the technophobes who came before us." I swung the apartment door open and dropped my bags in the entryway. "They probably got sick with the common cold but didn't have a phone to call for help. By the time their carrier pigeons got to town with their request for Tylenol and chicken soup, it was too late. Everybody was already dead."

Sam's smile could best be described as *polite.* "The people who lived here before us weren't technophobes." She crossed her arms over her chest and stepped inside the apartment. "We're pioneers that way."

"Right, yeah, I knew that. I was just joking." I kicked absently at my trash bag. "So, we'll be the first then. The first Luddites to die here of something preventable, and then *we'll* become the ghosts that haunt this place."

"Could be," she said. A note of disappointment softened her voice. I was beginning to realize she hadn't been joking; she genuinely wanted to talk about ghosts. "I don't even know how to operate a carrier pigeon."

"You have to wind it up first, I think."

"Totally."

Before I could ask what she'd meant about a haunting, Jack burst through the open doorway with an armload of boxes. When he saw Sam, he froze, staring at her like I'd smuggled her in my luggage from the life we'd come here to escape. He turned and hit me with his caged animal stare. "This is Sam," I said. My voice trembled. "She lives next door."

Jack's eyes didn't leave mine. "It's nice to meet you, Sam."

She said something polite in response before slipping out of the apartment.

As soon as we were alone, his eyes hit the floor. He hurried past me with his boxes and closed himself inside his new bedroom.

I stood alone in the entryway staring after him. He would deny it, probably, but the look my brother gave me when he saw me with Sam was the look someone gives a predator when they catch him coaxing a little kid into his van. It was a look that asked, "Are you going to bully this girl into killing herself too?"

II.

At dinner that night, we met the rest of the community's residents—Fish's husband, Brandon; their twin daughters, Sasha and Sarah; and Sam's dad, who introduced himself as Dr. Rimini. We were in The Castle's enormous dining hall, eight of us in a space big enough to serve hundreds. We were surrounded by long empty tables with no chairs. Our voices echoed with the wet sound of shower stalls and indoor pools. Jack and I shook hands with everyone, even the two little girls, then found seats at the only table that had been set. Brandon stood over a rolling cart, carving a roast. It smelled incredible. He was a chef who owned several successful midwestern restaurants, which explained their wealth. "So, Selbys, how are you settling in?" he asked. His energy was totally different from Fish's. Not a slick magician feeling at all. His vibe was more cookie-cutter businessman. Someone important. The kind of person you might call 'Sir' just because it suited him.

"All good so far," Jack said. He was eying everyone like we were at one of those murder mystery dinners, and he was trying to identify the killer. He paid specific attention to Sam, who'd taken the chair beside mine.

"Excellent," Fish said. He was seated at the head of the table. "You should spend some time fully exploring the grounds. Get to know every acre. We're all family here now." He winked at me as he brought his wineglass to his lips.

"What do you do for work, Jack?" Dr. Rimini asked, accepting a full plate from Brandon. He was tall with messy tufts of graying hair and a mustache. I wondered if Sam got her reddish hair from her mom. I wondered where her mom was.

"I'm a small business owner," Jack said. "Just starting out. I'm opening a freight brokerage with a buddy of mine."

"That's an important field," Brandon said, delivering two more plates. "Transportation is the backbone of any economy."

"Babe," Fish interrupted, "these glazed carrots look *eccezionalmente delizioso*." He emphasized those foreign words with an absurd Italian accent.

"*Grazie*," Brandon answered in a tone like an eye roll. The twins giggled.

"You're a doctor, you said?" Jack asked Sam's dad.

"A PhD in Religious Studies. I teach at Indiana University South Bend. Though, during the summer break, my vocation is author. I'm finishing a book. European and North American pagan mythology, that's my specialty."

"We're only three families strong," Fish marveled, "and already brimming with such fascinating characters."

"Dad," Sam said, "Milo's an oil painter too."

I didn't look at him, but I could feel Jack's eyes bore into me.

"Is he really?" Dr. Rimini asked. He seemed genuinely intrigued. "That's incredible. Are you any good, Milo? Sam's recent improvements have been remarkable."

Before I could respond, Jack said, "Milo used to be more into art than he is now. He's starting to move past it, right Milo?"

"Right," I said to my plate.

"Well, this would be the perfect place to rekindle his passion," Brandon said. "The Castle used to be an artist's retreat, after all." He set his own plate at the table and took a seat to my left, beside the twins. They were six or seven years old and whispering some secondary, private conversation.

"Of course, he will," Fish said, "and he'll have Sam here to encourage him." He clasped his hands like he couldn't be more delighted. "You see what I mean? Fascinating characters—a transportation professional, a writer, and our two young *artisti*." His Italian accent returned on the last word.

"My God, that accent…" Brandon said, shaking his head. "I expect each of you to make your dissatisfaction known when he starts showing off like this. I let it slide when we first got together, and now look what I've wrought upon myself."

"You let it slide because you found it charming," Fish said. "You did then, and you do now."

They went on in this way, like they were doing a bit for us, and got most of us laughing. Even Jack cracked a smile. It took the focus off me, which I was glad about. I hadn't had a well-cooked meal since Mom died, and after months of the processed garbage Jack and I had been living on, I wanted everyone to mind their own business so I could devour my food like a wild beast. We were only a few minutes into eating, though, when Brandon said, "Babe, it just occurred to me that in a few days we might end up with two artists *and* two writers."

Fish smirked at him. "Is this your way of telling me you've written a tell-all about our lives?"

"Don't tempt me," Brandon said. "I was referring to Roma."

"Oh, sweet Lord, that's even worse." Fish pantomimed blotting sweat from his forehead with his napkin.

"Who's Roma?" Sam asked.

"Roma," Fish said, "is Brandon's niece."

"She's likely going to take one of our vacant rooms," Brandon said, then added definitively, "but only for the summer."

"Assuming she doesn't get distracted by some motorcycle gang or activist group on her way to us."

"Darling…?"

Fish reached across the table and squeezed Brandon's hand. "Yes, dear?" They were leaning into each other but talking loudly, performing an intimate moment for our benefit.

"Will you do me a favor?"

"If it's in my power, then assuredly, yes."

"The next time you get the urge to gossip about my family in front of our new friends, why not smother that impulse in a giant bite of the delicious roast I made us?"

"But there's so much gossip," Fish said, "and so little roast."

Dr. Rimini howled.

Brandon returned his attention to the table. "Roma is my sister's only child. She's studying Journalism at Ohio State."

"Would you scold me again if I told them she was a firebrand?" Fish asked.

"No, I'd say that's flattering."

"Generous, more like."

Brandon ignored him. "Roma isn't getting along with her mom right now, so she's planning to stay with us during her summer break."

"I imagine the rent we're offering her looks pretty attractive after the family discount." He made a zero with his hand.

Brandon didn't respond. His eyes were fixed on Jack. In a scolding tone, he said, "This is a technology-free zone, Mr. Selby."

I realized he'd caught him sneaking a look at his phone under the table.

"Seriously?" Jack asked.

"Yes, seriously. It's a fundamental rule of our community. You know this."

Jack reddened, glancing around the table for someone to back him up. No one did. "You know," he said, "technically a knife is technology. And tables for that matter, and fire. We should all be sitting around naked, eating our raw food off the floor. No, wait—floors are technology too. We should be outside eating off the ground."

Fish and Brandon weren't swayed by his reasoning, and they let him know it with the gravity of their stares.

Beaten, Jack hid the phone in his pocket. "It's not like I had any bars, anyway. Is there even coverage out here?"

"Blessedly, no." Fish smiled and looked around the table. "Now then, who's ready for seconds?"

III.

"*Sleepy Baby, 1910.*"

"Hmm, I don't think I know that one. But if it's from 1910, and it's a painting of a baby, I'll guess Mary Cassatt."

"Ding! Ding! Ding!" Sam said, confirming I was right.

"I've never been a fan of pastel colors," I admitted, "so Impressionism isn't really my thing. There's one of hers I like, though. It's called *Sketch of Mrs. Curry*, I think…something close to that, anyway. It's a crude portrait of a dark-skinned woman. Weirdly, her body is overlaid with the upside-down face of some old white guy. Like, totally out of place and unexplained."

"That's a Cassatt?" She frowned like she couldn't imagine a famous painter of children making something like what I was describing.

"I know. It's bananas, coming from her. It looks like one of those old double-exposed ghost photographs. Like she painted a spirit projecting from the body of the sitter."

"I'll have to remember to look into that one…" Sam said. "Okay, you're up."

"Oh, sorry. Let's see, um…*Starry Night.*"

"Seriously, dude? Something challenging, please."

I held up my hands to say I hadn't meant any offense. I was sitting in her dad's recliner in their living room, hoping I didn't look as stiff and uncomfortable as I felt. No one had hung out with me in ages. "I wasn't trying to insult you," I said. "I think maybe I'm just crap at trivia." I rubbed the nape of my neck, thinking. After a moment, I had it. "Oh, I know! *The Portrait of Mr. and Mrs. Arnolfini.* I love this one! I can't believe I didn't think of it right away."

"Arnolfini…" she repeated slowly. I could tell she didn't know, and she was cycling through periods and painters hoping to work it out. Eventually, she voiced the sound of a buzzer to signal her defeat. "I give up."

"Jan van Eyck. You should check it out if you don't know it. It's simple at first glance, almost boring. It's deceptive, though. There's so much storytelling in the little details. To me it's like a reminder that nothing's ever quite what it seems on the surface, you know? I did a video about it on my channel." I immediately realized my mistake. My face went hot. I was a dumbass.

Before she could ask, we heard a door open down the apartment's short hallway. A second later, her dad appeared, scratching his balding head. I sat straight up to demonstrate we weren't doing anything untoward. Sam was sitting across the room, five feet from me, so I doubt it was necessary.

"Hey, guys," Dr. Rimini said, looking surprised to see Sam had company. "What are you two up to?"

"Just talking about art," she said.

He kneeled and grabbed a Gatorade from the mini fridge in their living room. With the communal dining situation, our apartments didn't really have kitchens, only a freestanding sink and a couple of tiny cabinets. "I came for electrolytes," he said, "and to stretch my legs. I feel for you, Milo. Sam's an encyclopedia of art. She'll keep you here all day if you let her."

"Milo knows more than I do."

"Is that right?" He gave me an appraising glance. "A painter and a scholar too. Good man, Milo."

"I don't know that much," I said.

"I'm curious, though—since you two share this passion in common, why are you just sitting here talking about it? Sam has supplies in her room. Go! Be creative! Make some art! Just be sure to shut your door, honey. I'm in the middle of a critical chapter."

Sam and I exchanged glances. I thought it was a pretty strange suggestion, to be honest. I mean, I was a teenage boy he'd literally just met, and he was inviting me into his daughter's bedroom. *And hey, kids, if it gets too hot in there, why not strip down to your underwear? It's just the most practical solution to the problem.* Dad used to say that academics had giant brains but no common sense. Maybe this was what he meant.

"I'm sort of on a break from painting," I said, "but I'd really like to see Sam's work."

"There's a ton of it," Dr. Rimini said. "Her progress has been remarkable."

I noticed her wince, but her dad apparently didn't. He just gave us a clueless wave before disappearing down the hall to close himself in his office.

IV.

"Before I show you my paintings, can I trust you with a secret?" We were in her bedroom, standing at a distance from each other on a shaggy, paint-splattered rug.

"Sure. I mean, who could I even tell, right?"

"Right…" She sounded uncertain. "First, tell me about your art channel. I saw on your face you didn't want to talk about it. Tell me, so we'll be even."

"I'm sorry, Sam, but I can't do that. I don't know what your secret is, but I can guarantee you it isn't the same kind of thing."

She stared at me, biting the inside of her cheek like she was debating how to proceed. Finally, she said, "You do have an art channel, though?"

"Technically, but I don't upload anymore." I avoided looking at her when I said this. My eyes moved instead over the stacks of canvases lining the floor and the work still drying on her desk and dresser. Finished paintings were laid out on virtually every surface of her room.

"Why don't you?"

"That's the part I can't talk about."

"Then I can't tell you my secret," she said, clearly frustrated but keeping her voice low on account of her dad.

"I get it. I'm sorry." After a few seconds of awkwardly standing there, blinking and not saying anything, I headed toward her bedroom door to go.

"Why is it just you and your brother?" she asked all at once, like she was groping for anything private I could tell her that would make her feel like she could trust me.

I stopped with my hand on the doorknob. "My parents died in a car accident a few months ago."

"I'm sorry."

"What about your mom?"

"Lung cancer. Last fall. She was a smoker."

When I'd first agreed to look at Sam's paintings, my plan was to keep things light. I would compliment her work, even if it wasn't any good; look at her art supplies; then I'd get out of there. So, this talk of cancer and car accidents was getting a little heavy for me.

"I just...I really need to tell this secret to somebody." She was staring at the door to her room rather than at me directly.

"Okay. I mean, I'm happy to listen."

"Will you tell me your thing though? It doesn't have to be now. But, whenever you're comfortable with it, will you tell me?"

"Sam...I'm never going to be comfortable doing that."

"Fine," she said. "Just...sit down while I tell you."

V.

"I'm terrible at oil painting. I mean, I draw well, and I'm good at watercolor—do you know John James Audubon?"

"Sure," I said. "Birds, right?" I was sitting on a stool beside her easel. Sam sat cross-legged on her bed.

"Right. He was an ornithologist, and he made a ton of paintings of North American birds. Mom loved him because she was an ornithologist too, so my whole life we had those Audubon bird books lying around our house. When I was younger, I got to where I could make pretty accurate watercolor copies of those paintings, so I naturally assumed I'd be good at oil too, you know? I already knew how to paint so what was the difference?"

I smiled along with her. "There's a huge difference."

"Oh, I figured that out... With oils, I could only make a mess. I kept trying though. When we arrived here, I was competent, but not skilled. That's important to know." She took a deep breath then slowly released it to make clear we were coming to the good part. "It started the day we moved here. By the time we'd carried in all our stuff and unboxed it, I'd walked up and down those stairs a hundred times, so I was pretty drained. The last thing I set up was my easel. By then it was, like, an hour before dinner, and I had the idea to paint a quick landscape of the grounds through my window. Like to commemorate our first day, you know?"

From where I was sitting, I could see through the same window. "It's nice," I said, appraising the view.

"It is. I thought painting it would make it feel like mine. But, as soon as I touched my brush to the paint, it was like…I'm not sure how to say this. It was like something took control of my hand. I painted so fast, and with so much confidence. I felt like I could have done it with my eyes closed."

I had been oil painting since I was thirteen, and I'd never had an experience like the one she was describing. I assumed she was bragging, trying to impress me. "You mean you felt inspired?" I asked, easing her away from those kinds of exaggerations.

"No," she said firmly, "that's not what I mean." She frowned and scratched her temple like she was trying to coax the words out of her brain with her fingernails. "This is going to sound pretentious and dumb, but it's the truth so I don't know how else to say it... While I was standing there painting, my thoughts focused on this little pinpoint of light in my mind. It's all I saw. Not the paint. Not the canvas. The light was everything. It guided my hand. Like my body had become an extension of it, or something. The longer I painted, though, the more the vision intensified, and I realized it wasn't a light at all. I started to see pockets of shadow inside it. Slowly, those shadows revealed themselves to be a face—Mom's I thought, at first, from her soft features. But then I saw her hair was different, short like a man's. Her eyes were closed, but they were enormous, not like Mom's at all. She was striking. She looked to be deep in concentration like she was connecting with me the same way as I was connecting with her. As she became clearer to me, I painted faster and faster. I was mixing colors on my palette, not even looking at the marks I was making on the canvas. I felt like I was on drugs or something—not that I've ever done drugs. My body was tingling, and my heart was pounding. She smiled, pleased with me. It only made her more beautiful. I had the sense I was just on the edge of achieving a perfect connection with her when I heard Dad call to me from down the hall."

"Shit..." I said. I had let myself get deep enough into her story that it felt like it was me her dad had interrupted.

"As soon as I heard his voice, the woman's eyes shot open. For a single second, she stared straight at me." She shook her head, remembering. "She looked so angry. And then she vanished from my mind. I dropped my brush and doubled over. I thought I was going to collapse."

"That's nuts."

"Right? But I got myself together with some deep breathing and this counting thing the therapist taught me after Mom died, and I finally looked at the painting I'd made. I'm not kidding when I say I was seeing it for the first time. Rather than the view from my window, it was this beautiful, complicated rendering of tenement houses, all cramped together on a filthy street. Clothes lines were strung between some of the buildings' windows, stories and stories above the ground. Hints of people were slumped on porch steps and hanging together in alleys. It looked like a frame from some classic film set in New York—which is a city I've never even visited." She got up from the bed and walked to a stack of canvases, flipping through them until she found it.

When she handed the painting to me, it was everything she'd described—gorgeous, intricate, masterful. "Sam, this is incredible!" I said.

She walked back to her bed then crouched and pulled out another canvas from beneath it. She gave it to me without looking at it herself. It was a portrait, even better than the cityscape. The sitter was a handsome woman with short hair which was shaved close on the sides. She was dressed in a man's dress shirt and tie. "God, the photorealism is insane! It's like looking at a photograph. Who is this of?"

"The ghost. The woman I see in my mind. She's been painting through me ever since that first day."

I glanced at her mountain of canvases. "All of these?"

"Most of them, yeah. And you're right. They're incredible. It's okay for me to say so because they aren't mine. She uses me, but it's her work, and I don't know how to stop her. She shows up every time I try to paint." Her eyes were brimming with tears.

I leaned the painting on the stool and stood up, facing her. "Can I see?" I asked.

"Sure," she said, sniffling. "Look at any of them you want to. It's mostly just landscapes, but there are a few abstract pieces too."

"No. I meant can I see you paint one?"

VI.

We set up our easels back-to-back, so we were facing each other, separated by the canvases between us. I couldn't see Sam except for her legs and the bit of hair that danced around the top of her canvas while she worked. I hadn't wanted to paint. I'd only wanted to watch her, but she said she wasn't a trained monkey, and she wasn't going to perform for me. I could understand that. I needed to see this phenomenon for myself, so I agreed to paint too.

I was holding a palette and a brush, but I was focused on Sam. I figured if her story was true and she went into a trance or whatever, I might be able to sneak over and watch without her realizing. I made some strokes on my canvas, aware of her hair bobbing around, listening to the scratch of her bristles as she worked. I pictured her face as if our canvases were a glass window I could see through, and I absently traced her onto that glass as I waited for the spirit to possess her.

Minutes passed. I mindlessly brushed paint onto my canvas, keeping my focus on Sam. As far as I could tell, no change came over her. So, I kept working, kept waiting.

"Milo!"

I snapped to attention.

"Milo!"

I looked to my left, and my body shuttered from the shock of seeing Sam standing inches away from me. Dumbly, I looked back across our easels like I expected to still see her there. "Sam?" I turned back to her, confused. She was staring at me with a harsh expression like I'd said something cruel or done something to offend her. "Sam, what's wrong?"

She didn't answer me, just shifted her eyes to my canvas. I did the same, and I struggled to understand what I saw. The painting was complete—a perfectly lifelike portrait of Sam at work, her brush pushed up against the canvas in a smear of bristles and paint, as if the viewer were looking at her through the canvas itself. On her face, I'd captured her expression of frustration when she realized her muse hadn't come. "When I walked over here, your eyes were rolled back in your head," she said gravely. "She connected with you this time, not me. Did you see her in your mind?"

I shook my head. "I only saw you." I stared at the painting for another few seconds, then I moved past Sam to have a look at her canvas. She voiced a small groan of apprehension, but she didn't stop me.

Casting my eyes over her work, I muttered an involuntary, "Oh…" She had painted a great blue heron. It was fine. Average. That's the best I can say. Sam didn't join me; she stayed where she was, in front of my easel, not speaking. I suddenly felt embarrassed to have outmatched her, and to have painted such an intimate portrait of her at a moment when she was clearly confused and upset. "I'm sorry, Sam," I said. I was just about to ask if she wanted me to go when a merciful knock sounded on her bedroom door. Dr. Rimini peeked his head into the room and said, "Hey you two, it's time for dinner." As fast as I could, I smiled and slipped around him, out of Sam's bedroom.

CHAPTER: 03

I.

Sam and I avoided each other for a few days. It might sound hard to do on a shared compound, but Jack was spending most of his time in town with Raj, which meant I was free to lock myself in my bedroom without him hassling me about it. Sometimes, I would see her from my window, strolling the grounds and looking lost in thought. She never showed up for dinner on the evening I painted her portrait. Dr. Rimini had come down without her, saying she didn't feel well. Brandon had offered his best wishes and fixed her a plate so she could eat upstairs. The same thing happened for two more nights.

Later that week, I was awoken by Jack pounding on my bedroom door. He yelled for me to get dressed, pronto. When I came out into the hall, he said, "You're going downstairs while I'm out today. I'm not going to have you turning into some shut-in weirdo."

Technically, he didn't ask me if I'd been spending all my time alone, so I didn't deny it. I didn't voluntarily admit to it either, though. "What do you mean?"

"Get your ass downstairs, Milo. You think I don't hear things? Everyone's going to start thinking you're a little creep if you stay locked away up here. It's weird. Don't be weird, all right?"

"Sure. Got it." We walked downstairs together, and he pointed for me to go into the common room. "It's empty," I said. "I could be by myself upstairs."

"Sorry, Milo. I didn't think to schedule you a playdate. Just sit there and read a book or whatever. Eventually somebody will come by and feel sorry for you and give you a pity hang." He shoved me in that direction then left without another word.

That's where I was, sitting on the couch and flipping through some book I'd grabbed from the fireplace mantle, when Sam came down the stairs. She started across the entryway but then saw me and stopped. We held like that for a second—me sitting with my eyes anchored to my book like I was oblivious to her, Sam sort of skulking around awkwardly. Eventually, she called: "How's my ghost working out for you?" Her voice echoed like a canyon lay between us.

I looked up at her, playing dumb. "What?"

"The ghost." She took a few steps toward me. "She left me. I mean, it was obvious she had when I saw your portrait. But I've started three different canvases to see if she'd come back. Everything I've made is trash. She's gone."

"Oh," I said, fidgeting with the pages of the book. "I'm sorry. That's…good, though, right? You acted like you were afraid of her."

Sam nodded, but her forehead was crinkled with uncertainty. "Does she come to you? Is your work still that good?"

My face flushed. "No—I mean, I don't know. I haven't been painting. I left my easel in your room, remember?"

She moved closer, stopping a few feet from me. "For real? Because it's okay. You can tell me. I mean, I miss having her talent. It actually really sucks to be this mediocre again. But it's fine. I'll get better. And you're right, she did scare me." She stared at me doe-eyed, awaiting my response.

"There's nothing I can tell you. Seriously, I haven't been painting."

She stared at me for long enough that I was starting to get uncomfortable. Still, I forced myself to stare right back at her. "That's so strange," she said before we were interrupted by the thundering sound of running and the squeal of high-pitched voices. I rose from the couch and, a second later, Sasha and Sarah came bounding toward us from the dining hall. Fish followed them, huffing.

"Girls," he called, "what did I say about running indoors?" He stopped when he saw Sam and me. The twins dropped to their knees at the coffee table between the couch and recliners. They'd brought blank paper and markers. "Milo," Fish said, greeting me. "And Sam! You're feeling better, I see."

"I am."

"Excellent news. I'm very glad to hear it. I was just dropping the girls here while I tend to some things in my office."

"Do you want to draw with us?" one of the girls asked me.

"Oh," I said, "that's really nice, but I can't."

"Why not?" Sam asked. "Do you have a date or something?" This made the twins giggle. "I'd love to draw with you girls. I think Milo should too."

"No, seriously." I stopped when I realized the twins were gawking at me, big eyed and open-mouthed. "I mean, I can stay, I guess. But I'll just watch you."

"Wonderful!" Fish said. "Girls, young Mr. Selby will be your creative director. Don't let up on them, Mr. Selby. Hold them to your highest standard." He squeezed my arm like we were sharing a joke. "You all have fun." He leaned into Sam and me and whispered, "Oh, and be forewarned—there's a rumor floating around that Roma is on the premises." His eyes were on the ceiling, dancing around like he was trying to detect her up there. "Should you run into her, my advice is to play dead."

II.

"It's a butt," said Sasha.

"It's *Sam's* butt," said Sarah.

"Interesting," said Sam.

I was sitting on a couch. They were all cross-legged on the carpet, drawing together at the coffee table. They were discussing the corkscrew shape Sasha had drawn on her construction paper. "I can see it, maybe, as *someone's* butt," Sam said. "The problem is, I've never seen my own because it's on the opposite side from my eyes."

"On the backside," said Sasha.

"The butt side," Sarah giggled.

"So you can't smell it." Sasha exploded into laughter.

Sam made a show of sniffing the air, flipping her hand in front of her face like she was drawing in nearby odors. "Hold on! I think I *can* smell it," she declared. "It smells…wonderful. Like fresh-baked cookies and," she pantomimed another whiff before adding, "peach cobbler."

"You're lying," Sarah said.

"Or she's in *denial,*" Sasha added, sliding her eyes to her sister for approval of this grown-up word before the pair of them erupted into a long laughing fit. I worried they might hyperventilate. Their howling mouths were all pink tongues and sporadic missing baby teeth. I smiled but only to be polite.

Eventually, they settled down and got back to drawing. Sasha adorned her expressionist take on Sam's posterior with other random shapes and squiggles. Sarah worked on the many claws of what I believed to be a tardigrade. Mostly, my attention was on Sam's drawing. It was a simple female figure. One with short hair and a solemn expression, wearing a collared shirt and tie. She'd sketched a remedial version of the portrait she'd shown me in her bedroom. I suspected she'd drawn it hoping the girls would recognize her, that they would excitedly tell all about how this same woman was haunting their bedroom. If those little kids had seen a ghost, though, I was certain we would already know.

When they didn't take the bait, Sam asked, "So, how do you girls like it here?"

"Fine," they said in unison. They did that sometimes. It was eerie.

"Have you seen anything weird since you moved in?"

"Fish is weird," a monotone voice answered from very near us—a stranger in the doorway, unnoticed until now. We all turned to look at her. She was breathtaking, tall and thin with spidery chandelier layers in her hair and eyes that were tipped down toward the bridge of her nose in a way that reminded me of some large-eyed goddess from Egyptian hieroglyphics. Looking at her, I had the thought that if The Castle wasn't already haunted by an elegant female spirit, this girl could certainly have filled the role. She scared the shit out of me from the very start. "I'm Roma," she said, as if she could be anyone else.

"Oh, hey," Sam said. "You're his niece, right?"

Roma snorted. "Fish? Not hardly. Brandon is my uncle, purportedly." Because she was standing, she towered over us. She stared at the coffee table with a look of detachment. I don't think she'd glanced at me even once.

I was no expert on girls, but I'd been picked-on enough in school to have an intimate understanding of the hierarchy of popularity. I heard a shift in Sam's voice when she spoke to Roma that I immediately recognized. It was a deferential thing, a signal to the Queen Bee that you accept her authority and will make yourself small to honor her grandeur.

"Oh, well, Brandon's cool," she said. "He's an excellent cook."

"What are you drawing?" Roma asked, ignoring her.

The twins had gone shy and said nothing. They sat stiffly with their eyes glued to their art. I guess that Queen Bee thing starts young. Like an older sister, Sam took the lead, going around the table: "Well, here we have a pretty excellent tardigrade, and then an interesting work of Expressionist art exploring the female form, and finally…well, I'm just sketching a woman, I guess."

"That's really good," Roma said. "Yours, I mean." Then, as if belatedly realizing the feelings of young children are easily hurt, she added, "And, I mean, the other ones too. The bear-thing and the shapes."

"Thanks," she said on behalf of them all.

"How do you know about her?" Roma asked.

Sam looked confused. "How does who know about who?"

"You, genius. How do you know about Florence Massey?"

Sam and I exchanged glances. "Who?" I asked.

"The woman in her drawing. You're telling me that's not Florence Massey?" When Sam didn't answer, Roma glowered at her like her silence was the most insulting kind of lie. "Whatever." She started to walk away.

"Wait!" Sam said and bolted to her feet. I rose too, more slowly, and we each weaved around the coffee table, approaching Roma from both sides. Sam presented the sketch to her like a homicide detective asking some scumbag to identify a Jane Doe.

Up close, her clothes were pungent with the sweet smell of cigarette tobacco. "I'm sorry, who are you?" she asked.

I told her.

She looked at Sam. "I don't know you either."

"Sam. You recognize the woman in this drawing?"

Roma arched her eyebrows, suggesting the question was absurd. "Yes, obviously. It's Florence Massey. The hair. The necktie. There's no one else it could be. So, what? Did you learn about her in a psych class or something?"

"No, I don't have psych. I'm in high school."

"Me too," I added.

"Super," Roma said, making clear she didn't care. She glowered at us, likely wondering why we were acting strangely.

"The thing is," Sam said, "I've drawn this woman before, but I have no idea who she is." She sounded embarrassed asking, but she did anyway: "Will you tell us how you know about her? Did this woman die here?"

Roma didn't speak right away. I think she was trying to work out if we were playing games with her. "No," she said eventually, "Florence Massey didn't die here. She died in a sanitarium in Paris in, like, 1950." She motioned for us both to lean in. The slightest smile raised one corner of her mouth. "Do you want to know how she died?"

I nodded and so did Sam, who turned her body slightly to block the twins from gaping at us from behind the couch.

"Well, it seems she had the unfortunate idea of stealing a 45-vinyl single of The Merry Macs', *Mairzy Doats* from her psych ward's music room. She sneaked it back to her cell, and sometime during the night, she broke it into slivers and stabbed one of them into her neck, right in the carotid artery. Her autopsy revealed multiple other vinyl splinters embedded in her skin from repeated missed attempts to hit the artery she wanted. She stabbed herself over and over until she got it right."

I felt the blood drain from my face.

"She didn't die here…" Sam said, wonderingly.

"Most definitely, she did not. Not even on the same continent."

Their voices sounded distant to me. I'd become light-headed. I was afraid I might pass out. My heart was hammering, and my fingers had gone numb. "I'll…be right back," I said.

Sam called out to me, sensing something was wrong, but I didn't answer. I hurried away from the common room. Thankfully, no one followed me. I gripped the railing all the way up the stairs, afraid I might fall. Somehow, I made it to my room before my body gave out.

III.

I don't know why I lied to Sam by telling her I hadn't been painting. Maybe I didn't believe she was actually fine with being mediocre again—I mean, how could anyone be fine with that? Or maybe I was just selfish, wanting to guard the work I was doing. The work *we* were doing, the spirit and me.

The truth was, since she'd followed me out of Sam's room, I saw her almost all the time. Not in my head, the way Sam described it, but walking around in the physical world. She disappeared now and then, but mostly she paced the floor of my bedroom, whether I was painting or not. I knew the mythology surrounding muses, how they would pair with artists to give them guidance and inspiration, but I'd always assumed it was superstitious nonsense—artists can be a superstitious bunch. Regardless, I couldn't imagine a more apt description of my relationship with her. She'd been Sam's muse, and now she was mine. I didn't feel great about it, but it's not like I'd stolen her on purpose.

Regardless, the feeling of painting with her was the first happiness I'd felt in months, and I had no intention of letting it go.

I couldn't say for sure whether Roma's story was true. The muse didn't speak, and the name Florence Massey didn't mean anything to me. Still, it was a lot, hearing about anyone dying so violently. I was unsettled by the possibility that she could be the ghost haunting my room. I guess it rattled me. I'd made it upstairs to the apartment just in time. I fainted or passed out, or maybe I just went to sleep to avoid confronting the possibility.

The first time the muse appeared to me, I'd been in bed, staring at my ceiling and thinking about Sam. This was after dinner on the night I painted her portrait. At that point, I wasn't sure exactly how I'd made something of such quality without even knowing I was doing it, but I wasn't buying her theory it was a ghost. I wasn't a skeptic, necessarily; I just tended to believe there was usually a rational explanation for supposedly paranormal occurrences. In this case, though, everything I came up with was at least as far-fetched as Sam's thinking. I was going over it again, looking for a reasonable answer and getting nowhere, when the vibe of the room shifted—a sudden electric charge in the air that left me certain Sam had been right all along.

It was kind of like when Jack and I first came to The Castle for our tour, the feeling of arriving somewhere I was always meant to be. In this case, it came as a sense of duty, like I was being called to some grand purpose I'd been specially built for. I rolled my head on the pillow to look out across the room, and there she was, staring at a stack of cardboard moving boxes. I wasn't afraid. I wasn't even excited. I just calmly sat up, walked over, and began ripping off the tape that held each box closed.

My art supplies were packed away in that stack, along with several dozen completed canvases I'd finished over the years. I'd left my good easel in Sam's room, but I had a spare—a cheap, metal one Mom had bought me when I was first getting interested in painting. I set it up and loaded it with an embarrassing still life I was happy to paint over, and we'd gotten to work right away. We made three paintings that night.

Together, they worked as a walking tour of the property. We painted the pond with its blue herons, then the woods beyond it—a wild, dark stand of trees in which a meandering path was visible only if you stared long enough for your eyes to find it. Finally, tucked into those woods, we painted the stone outbuilding with its rusty metal door. It was so detailed that names were perceivable, scratched into the rust. Most were faded, just like they'd been in real life, giving mere impressions of letters—vertical and diagonal lines mixed with rounded, circular shapes. In the painting, only one name was legible, as if it had recently been added—Sam Rimini. I felt the muse's cool breath on the back of my neck as we carefully drew each letter. I'd seen it written on the shed door during our tour, but I hadn't made the connection when I later met Sam in real life. Maybe it was because I assumed Sam was a man's name when I first saw it, or maybe I just wasn't the sharpest pencil in the box.

We'd painted more canvases since then. Each time, the muse had grown bolder, getting close enough for me to feel the tackiness of her skin against my back and arms as I stood at the easel, even through my clothes. I gave no thought to the paintings' subjects because the muse made those considerations for me. Often, the pieces were so abstract I couldn't tell precisely what I was looking at, even when they were finished. Still, I had no doubt they were perfect.

We were in the middle of another piece now, the seventh or eighth in that abstract series. I'd left Sam and Roma and blacked out, but I'd awoken to the muse coaxing me out of bed and over to the easel. I obeyed, taking an old portrait of Mom and Dad and covering it with gesso so something new could be painted over it. That's where I was, deep in a work trance, when my brain began to register a sound that was dull, hollow, and rhythmic like an echo from somewhere far away. My instinct was to fight against it, to stay focused. I tried to imagine my whole consciousness dropping into the center of the canvas where its network of shapes and colors could insulate me from the bother of that sound. But it didn't stop. Our work slowed. I was shocked back to reality when the muse forcefully withdrew her body from behind mine.

The feeling was like getting smacked on the back hard enough to steal my breath. My brush smashed into the canvas, leaving a smudge of imperfection.

The sound continued.

"What the hell?" I screamed, and as I turned away from the easel, I registered a frustrated look on the muse's face before she disappeared. I knew exactly how she felt.

The door. Someone was knocking on our front door.

I checked the time on my phone. Jack would still be at his work thing. Most likely, it was Sam. "Hang on!" I called.

To hide what I'd been doing, I would paint during the hours Jack was away from The Castle, and not again until after he went to bed. If he'd had any interest in me at all, he would have noticed the smell of oil paint coming from under my bed, but it turned out not to be a problem.

I crouched beside the bed now and gently pulled the edge of a paint-stained blanket from beneath it. As it slid toward me, it brought all our completed canvases into the open. I placed our latest piece among them, then hid them again by moving to the other side of the bed and dragging the blanket back underneath it. After wiping my hands on a rag dampened with mineral spirits, I jogged down the hall and unlocked the front door. I was standing in our kitchen nook with my soapy hands under the tap when I finally called, "Come in. It's open."

I heard the door unlatch, then Sam stepped into the apartment. "Hey," she said.

"What's up?" A soap bubble rose into the air and floated toward her before popping.

"So, what was the deal with your little freak out?" Right to the point.

"Oh, um…I don't know. I guess I'm not into scary stories."

"That much was obvious. I just figured I'd come by to make sure you weren't going all Howard Hughes on us."

"What does that mean?" I kept on scrubbing my hands.

"Howard Hughes? He was that old millionaire airplane guy. Isolated himself and became a germophobe? Probably had a sink that looked something like that." She gestured at the mound of suds overtaking my arms.

"Right, yeah." I felt caught, but I managed a weak smile. "I think I know him."

"You're acting kind of strange."

This was something I couldn't deny. Trying to make light of it, I grasped my chin in one soapy hand then pulled it away to reveal a King Tut-style bubble beard. I turned to her, mugging. "There's nothing strange about me at all," I deadpanned.

She nodded at my joke but fell short of a smile. "So…anyway. I had a conversation with Roma after you bolted."

I didn't want to hear this. I had no reason to trust Roma, and I had a very good reason not to get too deeply into this with Sam—chiefly, because it made me feel like a jerk to lie to her face. I turned off the faucet and grabbed the dishtowel to wipe my chin and hands.

"Guess what I found out? It turns out Florence Massey has a connection to The Castle."

"Oh, come on, Sam. How could Roma know that?"

"That's what I asked her."

"And?"

"And…she stared at me like she wanted to take a bite out of my face. She never did answer the question exactly. But I figure she's a goth journalism student who just moved into a historic building with an interesting past. It makes sense she'd look into it, right?"

"It's possible," I allowed.

Sam reached into her pocket and pulled out her sketch from earlier. When she unfolded it, I saw it was covered in handwritten notes. "Right, so do you know an artist named Sebastian Greely?" When I didn't respond, she continued, "Yeah, no one does. He was a friend of Dalí's—Salvador, I mean, obviously. Greely was the one who reopened this place as an artist's retreat. Guess who his companion was toward the end of his life."

"Florence Massey," I said without fanfare.

"Ding-ding-ding. And guess what else." The difference in our levels of excitement can't be overstated.

"I don't know, she was his muse?"

"Well, yes, he did call her that, but that's not what I was going to say. I was going to say the artist's retreat closed because Greely went missing. Like, for years. Until the 1960s when a hunter found his body buried on the grounds by the tennis courts. The guy's dog dug up the remains. Apparently, there were markings on the bones suggesting his throat was cut."

I made my face go skeptical the way Dad's sometimes did when I was little and exaggerating some story I was telling him.

"What…?" she asked, noticing.

"I don't know, Sam. I just kind of want to call bullshit on this. I mean, we'd know if a body had been found on this property, right? We both researched The Castle before we came here. She was probably just trying to scare you. And what about his art? Where are all the Sebastian Greely masterpieces we've never heard of? It doesn't add up."

"According to Roma, all his late work disappeared along with him, everything Florence would have been around for. We only know about it from Dalí and maybe a few others. They said it was great, though."

"According to Roma."

"Yes," she said, standing firm and ignoring every point I'd made. "There's something going on here, Milo. You know that. You experienced it yourself. This isn't so outrageous when you consider what we already know to be true, right? What I'm wondering now is— why did she come to me and no one else?"

I was unsure how to respond. Sam waited, her green eyes looking heartbreakingly vulnerable. Just over her left shoulder, the muse had materialized. Her head dipped slightly like she was taking in the smell of Sam's hair. Then she turned and walked slowly across the living room. Her expression was casual as if she'd only shown up to remind me she was watching. When she got to the hallway that led to my bedroom, she vanished. Sam never saw her.

"Earth to Milo."

"Sorry?"

"Why, do you think?"

"Oh, um…I don't know. I guess I'd need to think about it."

Sam nodded slowly. "Yeah, me too, I guess."

After a moment of awkward silence, I said, "So…"

Recognizing my stubborn refusal to be of any more help to her, she said, "Right. Well, then, I guess I'll go and let you get back to…whatever. Washing your hands."

I felt myself blush when she looked over to see the mountain of soap bubbles in our sink.

"But, hey," she said, "I told the girls I'd hang out with them again later since I ended up ditching them for Roma. You can come if you want. I figured we'd swim in the pond or dress up their dolls or play a board game or something."

"Yeah, I don't know. I don't really do dolls or dress up, I guess."

"Do you swim?"

"Poorly, honestly. But, even if I wanted to, Jack told me to have the whole place spotless by the time he gets home." This struck me as a serviceable lie to explain the sink situation. I moved toward the front door and was relieved when she followed me.

"I mean, it looks pretty clean, to me. Almost like you just moved in."

At the door, I shrugged and shook my head like, *Older brothers, what can you do?*

"Come down if you change your mind, though, okay?"

"Yeah, of course."

She paused before pulling the door open and stepping out into the hall. "Okay. I hope you do."

"Me too." I hit her with my friendliest smile then closed the door to her.

IV.

I quickly returned to work in my room. We painted for two more hours. By the time we finished, I'd forgotten about Sam's invitation to go swimming. I felt emotionally drained but keyed up too, like my body was electrified and out of sync with my foggy brain. I decided to go for a walk to burn off some of that leftover energy. I didn't think about Sam until I was out in the open field, just past the tennis courts. That's where I was when I heard her screaming.

The sound erupted from the tree line separating me from the pond and was immediately followed by a shocking explosion of birds scattering up into the sky. I didn't know if they were frightened by Sam's scream or by whatever had triggered it in the first place. Maybe it was both.

I'd like to say my instinct was to run to help them, to be the kind of guy who rides up on a white horse to save the damsels in distress—or, you know, some less sexist version of that guy. I was no hero, though. That's been established. Hero's journeys don't involve dead cheerleaders or stolen muses. Instead, my response was to freeze right where I stood.

For a few seconds everything was quiet. I started to convince myself that Sam and the girls were fine now. Maybe it was just a game they were playing. But more screams followed, words too distorted for me to decipher, unmistakable expressions of fear.

That's when my body unlocked, and I ran toward the pond. I heard splashing and yelling, and I saw flashes of movement ahead of me as I maneuvered between the trees, through the knee-high overgrowth that surrounded them. I heard other sounds, too, now that I was closer, sounds like wind rustling a flag or the roaring of a fire. I stabbed my ankle on a low branch when I tried to hop over a bush. I hobbled out into the grass surrounding the pond, and my attention immediately turned from the pain in my ankle to the scene ahead of me. There was a great blue heron at the edge of the water, enormous and desperately struggling to fly. It was flapping and flapping its huge wings but seemed to be held in midair three or four feet off the ground by some invisible magic. I realized this was the flag-waving sound I'd heard—the sound of the bird frantically trying to escape a pond which refused to let it go. I stared, trying to understand what I was seeing. I noticed the twins cowering together across the pond, upset and with their arms interlaced.

As I was about to shout to them, Sam called to me from a distance, "We need a knife!"

I turned to my right and saw her hurrying toward me, wielding a long stick. "What?" I asked.

"A knife, Milo. Do you carry a pocketknife?"

"A pocketknife? No, of course I don't carry a pocketknife. What's happening?"

She moved right past me as if to say, unless I could help her, I was wasting her time. "It's a fishing line," she called back to me. Her pace slowed as she neared the bird. "See?"

I took a few steps closer. The heron had fallen into a pattern of standing on a log at the edge of the pond then pushing off and struggling in the air before ending right where it started. After pausing, it would shoot up again like it was trying to escape its captor with the element of surprise. It took several of these attempts for me to see that every time it rose, a spray of pond water burst from under its right leg, spinning off an old fishing line that had snared it.

"I tried to stay as far away from her as I could and break the line down where it's caught on the log," Sam said, "but she freaked out. I couldn't get close enough. We need a knife or scissors." She jostled the stick in her hand. "I thought maybe I could break this and use the jagged end, but that's dumb, right?" She turned to me like she expected an answer. I realized she wasn't as in control of the situation as she first appeared.

"I mean, I don't know," I said. "I've never been fishing. I think those lines are pretty strong, though. I can run to the kitchen for a knife."

She gave a frantic nod before returning her attention to the bird, shushing and cooing at it. It squawked and flapped its monstrous wings and got nowhere.

The Castle was visible in the distance through an opening in the trees. I sprinted toward it, fast because I knew she might be watching, hoping if I was helpful now, it would lessen the guilt I felt for deceiving her. My lungs burned and my ankle throbbed. When I was only a few yards from the tree line, I passed by something glinting in the grass which caused me to circle back and drop to my knees. Digging it out of the earth, I felt soil cake under my fingernails. I imagined it packing so densely the nails would separate from my fingers and peel back. I had to shake the thought out of my head to keep working. When I felt the object loosen, I pushed all five fingers of one hand into the earth, grasping it. I pulled and pulled until, all at once, it came free, and I was thrown back onto my ass. I opened my hand to see a rounded piece of broken glass, the bottom of a beer or soda bottle. I sprung to my feet and brushed my thumb across its jagged edges as I ran back toward Sam. "This might work," I yelled when I was close. "I think this could cut it."

"Is it sharp?"

"Sharp enough, I think." She took it from me, and I bent over with my hands on my thighs, panting.

When I looked up, she had gotten close to the bird, cautiously inching toward it and then back, unsure how to go about the work of cutting the fishing line. She called, "Milo!" and I started toward her, afraid she would hand the glass back to me to face the wrath of the great blue heron myself. "She won't let me get close enough. You try." She held out the glass to me just as I'd feared.

"How am I supposed to…" I began, but she raised her palm in a clear sign my job was to stay quiet and take orders.

"Hold on a minute." She turned and rushed toward the twins, giving the bird a wide berth. Across the pond, the girls nodded along to whatever instructions she was giving them, then they rose together, collected the beach towel they'd been sitting on, and handed it over. She returned with the towel, muttering to herself as she approached me, talking herself through the finer points of how to proceed. "We have to swaddle her with this," she told me, gravely.

It would be an exaggeration to say the bird was as big as we were, but that's the impression it gave. "I don't know how we'd do that."

Sam took a step away from me and held out the towel with both hands, mentally comparing its size against the size of the bird. The towel was long enough to wrap completely around its body but too narrow to cover both its head and its long legs. To do what she was planning, a choice would need to be made: swaddle its lower half and deal with its sharp exposed beak or cover its head and body and risk the punishment of its uncovered legs. Sam chose the latter. She headed toward where the heron was perched on the log, speaking to me and the bird in the same singsong voice. "It's okay, honey, we just want to help you. When I have her secured, Milo, you need to cut the line as quick as you can. Milo's going to cut you free, baby. Okay, Milo, get ready on the count of one…two…*three*." She tossed the towel over the bird's head just as it was about to leap into the air again, then she lurched forward and hugged it, holding it tight enough to prevent its escape. Her body jerked as the heron thrashed and fought her. "Now, Milo, now," she sang with a new, panicked note in her voice.

For once, I didn't hesitate. It wasn't bravery; I think it would be impossible for anyone to witness the danger she'd just put herself in and not feel called to help. Hurrying to the cold shallows of the pond's bank, I stepped into the water and braced my knee on the log. I bent forward, grasped the fishing line and began attempting to saw through it. Repeatedly, the glass slipped, plucking the line like a guitar string. I turned it from edge to edge, trying to find the sharpest point. "Hurry

Milo!" Sam said urgently. She was holding the heron more awkwardly now, like it was a weight that was becoming too much for her to handle. Its right wing had worked free from the towel and was waving uselessly. A portion of the bird's head was exposed, and one yellow eye stared in my direction. "Please," Sam hissed.

I shook my head to refocus then got back to work on the line. I sawed at it furiously until my shoulder began to ache. I thought of abandoning the glass entirely and going at the line with my teeth, but then I felt it finally dig in. In only two or three passes, the line snapped, and I fell forward, slamming my chest against the log and losing one hand up to the wrist in the cool mud surrounding the pond. At that same moment, Sam let out a startled squeak. I glanced up just in time to see her hit the ground, hard. The heron had gotten free. It briefly rose into the air, but the towel weighed it down. The bird landed in the grass as inelegantly as a crashing plane, then it worked itself free and flew up into the sky and over the tree line. It was gone in seconds. The pond was suddenly quiet, like it had never been there at all.

I let out one of those involuntary rollercoaster screams, an adrenaline sound of delight mixed with horror. In the distance, the twins yipped and clapped.

It took some effort to pull my hand out of the muck, which seemed to pull more firmly the harder I struggled. Finally, it released me with a spluttering sound which seemed so undignified in that moment of triumph, I had to laugh. "Are you okay?" I called out to Sam, expecting the answer to be yes, expecting her to be elated, just like me. She didn't answer, but I heard one of the twins calling, "Sam? Sam, are you okay?" The fear in that tiny voice was like a hypnotist snapping me to attention. I rose out of the pond to find Sam lying in the grass, arms hugging herself, staring into the sky. Her knees were raised, but her legs were spread like they'd fallen to either side under their own weight. Snaking lines of blood ran down the skin below her shorts, too many to count.

What happened next is a blur. I remember my foot on the log, propelling me forward. I remember standing over her, staring down and seeing the rips in her shirt from where the bird's talons had torn into her. I remember the shutter of her body when she exhaled. I remember blood. I remember yelling at the twins to stand back to give her space. I remember running quickly across the grounds, back to The Castle. I remember yelling answers to the 9-1-1 operator's questions over the landline.

CHAPTER: 04

I.

The twins were exuberant, going on about the size of the bird to Fish and Brandon, apparently still high on adrenaline. Sam was sitting in the open back doorway of an ambulance. Her legs dangled over its bumper. She was perfectly calm, chatting with the EMT who was examining her cuts and scratches. I was standing nearby in the horseshoe-shaped driveway, being inspected by a second EMT, even though I'd told him the heron never touched me. He'd said he needed to be sure and instructed me to take off my shirt. When I'd refused, he'd said, "Birds are no joke, son. Ever hear of E. coli? Salmonella? Staphylococcus? Birds carry all that. Also, lactobacillus, Pasteurella multocida, proteus, you name it." I agreed just to shut him up, pulling my T-shirt over my head to stand tits-out for all the world to see. Dr. Rimini was waiting in his Prius behind the ambulance. They needed to sterilize her wounds immediately, they'd said, but she would still need to go to the hospital to have the worst of them irrigated. He was waiting to follow them with his engine running.

When I'd guided Sam up to The Castle from the pond and explained it all to him, he'd shaken my hand and thanked me for taking such good care of his daughter. I didn't bother explaining how little I'd done, how Sam was the only hero here. Jack probably would have pointed it out, but he was still in town with Raj.

"You sure made fans out of those little girls," the EMT was saying to Sam, probably trying to distract her from the pain of whatever she was rubbing into the scratches on her legs. "I can't stand birds, myself. If it had been me that found it, it would have stayed hung up until it starved. My nana had a bird, a big tropical one she would let roam free around her house. It was so hateful to me when I was little, screaming and pulling my hair with its beak and grabbing at me with its little claws."

"That would be scary for a kid," Sam said. "I've always thought birds were cool, though. My mom used to study them, so I guess that's why. But I know a lot of people think they're bad omens."

"Sounds right to me." The EMT scowled. "Nasty, dirty things."

"Mom told me some cultures believe they hang around us because it's their job to lead departing souls to the afterlife. That can make people wary of them. But there are other cultures that think our souls actually turn into birds when we die, so they honor them and feed them and everything. I like to think of them that way."

"Well, if that's true, then I guess you saved a soul today… Oh, sorry, does that sting too much?"

"It's fine." She let out a long, slow breath like maybe it really wasn't so fine. After a moment, she said, "We used to have finches in the eaves of our old house. They'd come every summer. Mom called them our fat squatters. When she got sick and couldn't talk anymore, we set up her hospice bed in the living room, and she'd lie there and stare at them all day. You could always hear them chittering outside the picture window, and I used to imagine she was talking to me through those birds, saying 'hi' or 'do your homework' or whatever."

I'd been eavesdropping on their conversation only to distract myself from the embarrassment I felt standing there half-naked, but Sam's story about her mom caused me to perk up.

"That's sweet. And you all moved out here when your mom passed?"

I wasn't looking at her, but Sam must have nodded.

"Well, I'm sorry that's what brought you, but this place has always been beautiful to me. I grew up right over there past those woods. We used to sneak out here when we were in high school. It was empty then, so we figured we weren't hurting nothing."

"That's cool. What was it like then?"

"Oh…about the same, as far as I can see. The grass was overgrown. It looks cleaner now. We never came up here to the house. We weren't vandals or anything. We'd just party out by the pond. We mostly came at night, so I never saw any birds like the one you got into it with today, which was fine by me."

"I wouldn't want to be alone out here at night. Especially if it was abandoned and broken down."

"Yeah, it was spooky, don't get me wrong. But we were young and senseless. The scariest part was that we passed this little building in the woods on the route we took from our street. It reminded me of a fairytale house made of stones. But I remember it had this bright orange metal door. It was all rusty, you know? If you ran your fingers down it, they'd get all orange from the rust. The boys would always act tough, trying to break into it, but no one could ever jimmy it open. My sister told me that's where Frankenstein lived, and it creeped me right the eff out. I'd always run as fast as I could past it, and she'd laugh and laugh." The EMT laughed, herself, at the memory. "Is that old building still out there?"

Surprising me, Sam answered, "I'm not sure. I don't think so. I've not seen a building like that."

II.

I didn't get a chance to talk to her before they drove her away in the ambulance. If I had, I'd have asked why she lied to the EMT. Sam and I had never talked about the stone building, but she must have known about it because she'd scratched her name onto the door. Something about it didn't sit right with me. I was keeping my own secrets, so I had no right to judge. Still, it stuck around like a whisper in the back of my mind.

With everything settled—Sam and her dad off to the hospital, Fish and Brandon inside with the girls—I decided to return to the woods for another look at the building. I took off through the field with the stupid conviction I was solving some great mystery. At least, I could confirm I wasn't crazy, that it really was *Sam Rimini* carved into the rust.

When I arrived at the pond, I saw the little circle of glass sitting on the log where the great blue heron had been snagged, and it hit me again how scary it was. I picked up the glass and kept an eye on the pond as I walked around it like it might sneak up and drown me if I let my guard down.

Stepping into the woods, I realized I wasn't entirely sure how to get where I was headed. I'd found the building last time by accident. From the painting we'd made of this section of the woods, I knew the path leading to it was tricky to find. After roaming around for longer than I would like to admit, I finally found the building tucked behind two giant elm trees. I hiked through tall brush to the front side and moved a drooping branch out of my line of sight. Right there in the middle of the door, just above the metal handle was her name, clear and freshly carved—*Sam Rimini.*

I'm not sure, I remembered her saying, *I've not seen a building like that.*

If I'm being honest—and at the time, I don't think I would have admitted this to myself—I'd mostly come out to see if my own name had shown up alongside hers. I just couldn't picture Sam lying about anything at all, let alone something as meaningless as an old shed. So, if she was telling the truth, and she really didn't do this herself, I had to wonder if it was the muse who'd carved it. If so, my name should have been there too, right? I mean, sure, she had chosen Sam first, but now she was mine. My name should be the biggest and clearest of them all.

I searched the door from top to bottom, but it wasn't there. My name was nowhere to be found.

Disappointed, I ran my finger down the front of the door. It didn't leave a mark in the rust, but my fingertip came away orange, just like the EMT said it would. I shifted the curved glass in my hand to get a comfortable grip, then I chose a spot right in the center and scratched my name in giant letters. I stepped back to appraise my work. It was legible, but faint. I tried again, pressing harder, going over the same lines. Even then, it was nowhere near as clear and defined as the smaller *Sam Rimini* beneath it. I got pissed then and went over and over every line like a madman, getting sloppy, cutting outside the original lines, upset that it wasn't making any difference. A bark of frustration escaped my throat, and I shifted from my name to Sam's, scratching the glass back and forth over it, trying to make it disappear. The marks I made were even fainter than the letters of my name. I barely scuffed it at all. Friction caused the glass to grow hot in my hand, and then it broke into two pieces and sliced across three of my fingers. I cursed into the trees. My voice echoed across the pond.

I pitched the shards into the brush, and a few fat drops of blood flung after them. Grabbing the door handle with my bloody hand, I pulled it as hard as I could. The gritty rust on the handle stung the cuts on my fingers, but the door didn't budge. I pressed my fingertip to the keyhole, wondering if any key still existed to unlock it, then I tried the handle again, this time with both hands. The blood on the handle caused me to slip, pulling open the cut skin on my fingers. I howled in pain, waving the hand in front of me, fingers splayed, splattering tiny red drops onto my shirt and the rusted door and the overgrowth surrounding me. When the stinging finally lessened, I examined the cuts to see how bad they were. I doubted they were deep enough to need stitches, but they were open and filthy with dirt and rust. I felt like an ass, like a raging baby. No one was around to see my tantrum, but I was embarrassed of myself anyway, like the woods themselves were watching and judging me. I needed to clean myself up, find bandages. Before I left the woods, though, I stepped back up to the orange door and added my name to it in glistening red.

III.

Sam and her dad didn't make it back in time for dinner. Jack got home just as the rest of us were sitting down at the long dining table. He sniffed around Roma for a few minutes but didn't ask about the missing Riminis. It came up, of course. Fish and Brandon launched into the heron story almost as soon as we sat down. As they told it to Jack, the twins chiming in here and there to provide their expert witness commentary, his jaw clenched and flexed. I sat across from him, knowing for sure which pieces of information he was mentally underlining—Milo, bloody girl, accident, ambulance, hospital. When their story was over, he looked at me in a way that suggested I was the lowliest predatory piece of garbage he had ever seen. He seemed to miss the part about me calling 911 and helping Sam limp all the way back to The Castle. I could have told him Dr. Rimini shook my hand for doing all that, but that same hand was now covered in Band-Aids, so I figured it was probably better not to draw his attention to it.

"Do you think we should do something about those herons?" Brandon asked Fish. "We can't have them injuring our residents."

"Great blue heron attacks are rare," Roma said. This was her first contribution to the conversation. "Unless you startle them or get too close to their nests."

"Yes, I'm sure that's right," Fish said, looking at her like he was surprised to agree with her about anything. "They're majestic. The bird was in duress. It didn't know Sam was trying to help it."

"Well," Brandon said. "At the very least, I think the pond should be off limits to the twins."

Sasha and Sarah whined their objection.

"Oh," Fish said, "you're just a worrywart. What happened today was a freak accident. The girls will continue to go to the pond, and they'll be just fine." He patted the hand of the twin nearest to him. "Now, what do you say we change the subject to something more pleasant?" He looked around the table. "Jack! How was your day? Do you bring us any news from the outside world?"

"My day was fine." He was eating slowly, and his eyes kept returning to me.

"I know," Roma chimed in, "why don't we talk about the ghost that lives here?"

Fish and Brandon shared a glance before joining the rest of the table in staring at her. "Ghost?" Fish asked.

"Sam told me she saw a ghost in her bedroom. She showed me a sketch of her she made. Did you two disclose to your tenants that the building was haunted?"

A mischievous grin bloomed across Fish's face. I noticed it at the same time as Brandon, who seemed to realize his husband was about to say something unhelpful and tried to stop him by speaking up himself. "Roma," he said, "it's a myth that landlords are required to disclose rumors of paranormal activity to prospective renters. Not that we would hide such a thing ourselves. And it makes no difference anyway because this building isn't haunted. There are no such things as ghosts." He smiled at us reassuringly.

Jack was growing visibly upset. I had to look away from him.

"Well put, dear," Fish said, then he sat forward with his elbows on the table. "What I want to know, though, is what precisely Sam thinks she saw. What did she say about her ghost?"

"Don't encourage this..." Brandon said.

"She told me the ghost is a young woman who wears a necktie and a man's dress shirt. She said she was her muse."

I felt a prickle of jealousy. "*Used to be* her muse," I wanted to say.

Fish clapped his hands together, delighted. "A muse!" he cried. "How wonderful! Our own muse! And a spectral drag king at that!"

"Fish!" Brandon scolded. "You'll scare the girls. Roma is obviously just having fun with us."

"Oh, yeah," Roma said flatly, "With you guys, I'm having so much fun."

"On behalf of us both," Brandon said, "let me reiterate that, while my husband has a playful sense of humor, neither he nor I know anything about this or any ghost. Correct, Fish?"

The mood at the table had become tense. We were all waiting for Fish to answer. He held his gaze on Roma. His face had a quizzical look. Finally, he blinked and smiled. "Of course. I'm sure Sam only saw a shadow. With as much atmosphere as The Castle has, it's a wonder we aren't all seeing things."

"She said Milo's seen her too."

"Okay," Jack said, bolting up from his chair, "I've had enough of this. I'm going upstairs. Milo, come on." He stormed out of the dining hall, through its heavy double doors. I looked down at my lap, aware of the entire table watching me, then I pushed out my chair and followed him.

IV.

Jack didn't lay into me that night. He didn't yell, and he didn't hit me. When I walked into our apartment, he just turned on me, wagging his finger in my face, and hissed, "You keep away from those girls, Milo. Do you hear me?" Then he marched off and disappeared inside his bedroom, slamming the door behind him.

When I opened my bedroom door, the muse was standing at my easel. She startled me, even though, by then, I should have expected her. My head was just somewhere else, I guess. I turned out the light and dropped my gaze to the floor, pretending I didn't see her. I didn't have it in me to paint; the day had been too upsetting. I got into bed, facing the wall. I could feel the cold presence of her standing at my bedside, watching me. A shiver went up my body when I felt the mattress take her weight as she lay down beside me. My heart began to race. She'd never done this before, gotten so close to me, other than when we were working. I waited for a long time, but nothing happened. She didn't reach to comfort me or whisper my name. Still, it was a tender moment, like she was protecting me. Or maybe she just wanted to be near me. Eventually, I rolled onto my back, and for a few minutes, I blinked up at the ceiling. The muse shifted beside me. I took a deep breath and said, "Florence?" It was the first time I'd called her by that name. I turned to face her then froze in fear. Her mouth was open in a silent scream, a black gaping maw of pain and anger. Her eyes were rolled back in her head, her eyelids fluttering. Her body began to pulse like she was in the middle of a seizure. "Florence?" At the sound of her name, her head turned toward me, slow like it was being pulled by gravity rather than by her own will. Her expression never changed. She stilled then, gaping at me for one second, two, three, before, all at once, she heaved toward me, her body landing on top of mine, chest to chest, face to face. Her weight took my breath. I struggled to escape her. Before I could, her body slackened. Her weight lightened. I felt panicked by her impossible closeness to me, her body melting into mine, disappearing into me. I remember feeling the pressure of her inside my chest, awful and incredible, before everything went black.

V.

I think of this as the night Florence started giving me visions. But then I remember the dream I had back home in Muncie after we returned from our tour of the grounds—the dying woman and the finches. Was it a vision of Sam's mom, or just a nightmare I've applied meaning to after the fact? Part of me thinks it was Florence who showed me that scene, that we shared a connection from the very start. A larger part of me finds this idea to be horrifying.

At any rate, after I blacked out, my awareness opened into a small room with garish fluorescent lighting. The steady beep of a heart monitor made me understand we were in a hospital room. I saw Dr. Rimini sitting in a chair, flipping through a magazine. Then, I turned to see Sam in a paper gown, sitting up in a hospital bed and scrolling on a phone. I say I saw her, but the experience was more than that. I was seeing her, facing her, but I could feel her too. I watched her scratch at the bandages on her arm, but I also felt the itch on her skin, and I shared her thought—not quite fully formed into words—that she had to be careful not to start it bleeding again. I had no thoughts or feelings of my own. I was only able to observe and receive from Sam.

She was waiting for the nurse to come to irrigate her wounds, delighting in her father's phone and the guest Wi-Fi, the first Internet connection she'd had since moving to The Castle. She logged into her old email accounts and sent a few messages to friends. She looked up a couple of influencers she used to follow. Then she went to YouTube and typed in, "Milo Selby." She found none of my videos in the top results—some skateboard trickster shared my name and was clearly the more popular poster—but my videos weren't too hard for her to find. She scrolled to the one on *The Portrait of Mr. and Mrs. Arnolfini,* and she watched it to the end.

She loved it. I felt her love for it. As a presenter, she found me charming in a cocky, big-brained sort of way. She liked what I revealed about the painting—hidden meanings in what appeared at first to be a boring portrait.

She watched more videos, including a few where I made my own paintings. None were as good as my portrait of her, not even close. Still, she would have watched my channel in real life had she known about it. So, why had I abandoned it? She began to scroll through the comments of the video she was watching.

The initial responses were more than a year old, posted shortly after the video dropped. They were lighthearted and complementary. Probably from kids who knew me, she guessed. Nine months later, though, a new spate of comments had appeared in greater numbers. They were severe in tone. The first of these contained only a single word: *Murderer!!!* It was so ugly and unexpected it caused her heart to hammer in her chest. She brought the phone close and read through every comment after that one. There may have been seventy-five, some defending me, but many flat out accusing me of killing a girl. Most posts called her Rebecca, and several, RS, but one gave her full name—Rebecca Steiner.

Sam Googled her name and Muncie Indiana. The search returned a page of local news stories about the death of "the homecoming beauty," which is what the headlines called her. She'd died three months earlier. The same school photo accompanied each article, and in it the girl really was beautiful, or at least very pretty—wavy brown hair and hazel eyes and a perfectly straight, white-toothed smile. Looking at the articles' datelines, she found it had only taken a few days for the news to shift from characterizations of her "unexpected death" to her "tragic suicide." Subsequent articles changed focus from Rebecca's death itself to the cyberbullying that was believed to have contributed to her "compromised state of mind." One of her classmates, an unnamed male, was expelled from their high school for an "inappropriate and hostile" message he'd posted about her online.

Was I the unnamed male?

Sam supposed I had to be, but it didn't make sense to her. I was no one's idea of cool. Rebecca, on the other hand, was the homecoming queen. In the social caste of any American high school, she would have been miles outside my league. *So how could someone like me bully someone like Rebecca?*

Back on YouTube, she entered our names together, "Milo Selby + Rebecca Steiner." The top result was a video that turned out to be a cringy memorial in which four of Rebecca's friends—a *Charlie's Angels* crew of diverse high school beauties—harmonized some sad R&B song Sam didn't know. She paused it halfway and scrolled to the comments, and that's where she found what she was after. The individual accounts of what happened were scattered and incomplete, and they didn't always add up, but after reading through all the comments, a basic story emerged.

Rebecca and I were classmates. Depending on who left the comment, I was either a forgettable nobody or a school shooter in training. Rebecca was both a saint and a full-fledged Mean Girl. I had either been terrorized by her and her friends for years, or else I'd developed a creepy crush and wanted to punish her for being out of my grasp. Everyone agreed she'd posted a comment on one of my art videos—Sam searched for that video but, unsurprisingly, it had been taken down. A few commenters, though, recalled what she'd written as, "OMG! Milo is such a geek. Why would ANYONE watch this trash??"

Unfortunately, I'd replied to her. One user recalled what I wrote as, "If I were as vapid as this girl, I'd kill myself." Not great, Sam thought, but not as bad as what another user claimed I wrote, which was, "Bitch, kill yourself now. I have some turpentine you can swallow." The use of the word "vapid" made Sam suspect the first post was the real one, but she couldn't know for sure. Either way, two weeks later, Rebecca took her own life.

After her death, Sam learned, my comment was reported to school administrators. I was expelled and, she correctly presumed, driven into hiding at The Castle.

By the time she finished reading every comment on every available video, she was under the hospital bed's covers, on her side and curled into herself like a baby. The scratches on her stomach hurt. She watched more of my videos, hoping to see a flicker of which boy I was—the picked-on kid who made an offensive joke at the expense of a popular girl who no one knew was quietly suffering, or the monster who taunted the homecoming beauty to death. She didn't see the monster in me, but she wasn't stupid. She knew monsters sometimes hid behind friendly smiles and bright eyes. But Sam also knew how mobs could create fictions that amplified outrage. Whether their weapons were torches and pitchforks or mean tweets, a mob was a mob. She'd learned that from her dad, who never missed a chance to preach against social media.

When the nurse finally entered the room, she walked straight through me on her way to Sam's bed. Sam closed out of YouTube and put the phone on the rolling table beside her. She still didn't know which version of me was real. She decided to give me the benefit of the doubt until she learned if I was a monster or just a boy who made a mistake that would haunt him forever.

VI.

I woke up gasping for breath. I'd been shocked awake by nightmares before, but this wasn't like that. It was a feeling like I'd been dropped from a twelve-story building, and I regained consciousness just as I slammed into my bed. I pawed at my chest, groping for the heaviness of Florence, that foreign body inside my own. Everything seemed normal, though. The obstruction of her was gone. I was on my back, my chest heaving. When I blinked, I could still see a ghost halo from the fluorescent lights in Sam's hospital room. I looked to my right and froze at the sight of Florence sitting on the edge of my bed. Her back was to me. She turned her head a little like she'd heard me stirring behind her. She never looked at me, though. She just slowly rose and walked across my bedroom floor, past my easel, then disappeared through the exterior wall.

I scurried out of bed and switched on the light. I had a desperate urge to get as far from my bedroom as possible.

The hallway was dim when I opened my bedroom door. I stood in the doorway, listening until I confirmed the sound of Jack's snoring. I sneaked past his room then grabbed my shoes, carrying them into the outside hall before slipping them on.

The first floor was dark when I started down the staircase, like everyone had gone to bed, so I just about jumped out of my skin when I ran into Dr. Rimini on the first-floor landing.

"Milo!" he said, sounding startled, himself. "What's the hurry, did you see a ghost?" I'm sure he meant it as a joke.

"Sorry, I just…I couldn't sleep. Is Sam okay?"

"She's just fine." He clapped me on the shoulder before continuing up the stairs. "Me, on the other hand? I'm worn out and ready to put this day behind me. Don't get old, Milo. It's not as glamorous as they tell you." I stood on the landing until he disappeared beyond the second-floor railing.

I didn't question why the front doors were unlocked. I just pulled one open and was confronted with the pungent smell of cigarette smoke. I stepped outside, momentarily confused.

"Well, well," Roma said, "now it's a party."

I looked to see her sitting cross-legged against one of the giant stone columns, the ember of her cigarette dancing with the movement of her hand in the darkness. Sam was standing beside her. "Hey, Milo," she said. Her voice sounded reserved and hesitant. I'd have been hesitant to talk to me too if I'd just learned about me what she had.

"Hey," I said, taking a few steps toward them.

"You know," Roma said, "when Brandon offered to let me stay here, the thing he kept emphasizing was isolation. 'It's total isolation,' he said. Yet I come outside for a smoke, and I've suddenly got a hospital mummy coming at me from one side and this spooked little rabbit from the other." She took a long drag. Her face lit up behind the brightened ember.

"I don't look like a mummy. It's not like I'm wrapped in bandages."

"I'm down here with your legs, cutie, and I beg to differ." Then, to me, she called, "Did your brother beat the shit out of you after dinner or what? You look like hell. Sorry if that was my fault."

I came to join them. "No," I said, trying to act like I hadn't just experienced the scariest few minutes of my life. "he didn't touch me. And it wasn't your fault."

"Why would he beat you up?" Sam asked.

"Because he's a dick as far as I can tell," Roma said. "I was telling them about your ghost at dinner. I think it set him off."

"You told them about Florence?" I couldn't see her well, but it was clear from her voice that it upset her.

"Oh," Roma said, "so now you believe me about Florence Massey?"

"I never said I didn't believe you. I just...I don't know...I don't think it should be open conversation, I guess."

Roma scoffed. "Brandon and Fish are clueless to anything but their own money and luxury. You could give birth to a zebra right in front of them, and five minutes later all they'd be thinking about is some imported Italian butcher-block table they're coveting."

"How do you know all that about her?" I asked. "About Florence Massey and her connection to this place?"

"You believe me too, huh?"

Sam glanced at me. I shrugged to say I had no idea what to believe.

Roma brought her cigarette to her lips and took a long drag, letting the smoke roll slowly out of her mouth. "I looked into it, that's all."

Sam took a step back from the cloud of smoke, making a quiet but audible throat-clearing sound. "Looked into what?" she asked. "I researched The Castle before we moved here. Milo did too. We never saw anything about a body, or any of what you said."

"You," Roma said, pointing the lit end of her cigarette at her, "seem like a nice enough girl. But, as a researcher, maybe you're not so impressive." I got the feeling she'd noticed Sam's attempt to distance herself from the smoke and was now gesturing with her cigarette to taunt her. I remembered her mother's lung cancer.

"Screw you," she said, which was uncharacteristically aggressive for Sam. In fairness, she'd had a rough day.

Roma chuckled. "That's a pass, doll. I'm not into children. Ask me again in a few years and maybe we'll reevaluate."

It was too dark for me to see if Sam was blushing, but I blushed on her behalf.

Roma stubbed out her cigarette in the soil of a potted plant. After a moment, she asked, "You've really seen her?"

"In my room," Sam confirmed.

"Why should I believe you?"

"It's not important if you believe me or not. I'm just curious how you know so much."

"Fair enough…but I already told you—research. I'm a journalist. All the information I found was right there if you'd bothered to go deeper than Wikipedia. And to answer your question, the reason I investigated it was because I got curious when Brandon bought the property. When I get curious about things, I do research. Media's a patriarchy. To succeed in the field, a woman needs to be the most knowledgeable, prepared person in the room. This was just practice for later, when I take over the world."

"Fine, but you told Sam that Florence Massey killed that guy and buried his body on the property."

"Sebastian Greely," Sam said.

"Right, and there would obviously be a Wikipedia entry if a millionaire's body was discovered on the property. It wouldn't be something you'd have to dig to find. It would be common knowledge."

A broad Cheshire Cat grin grew across Roma's face, suggesting this was exactly what she would have expected a dipshit like me to think. "Well, number one, I only *implied* Florence killed Sebastian. That's a theory of mine. It's not in the official history, because I'm the one who thought of it. Number two, Greely's family was rich, and they kept the nature of his death low key to avoid a scandal. There's one *Post-Herald* interview with the hunter who found the body, though. It got out before the family took control of the narrative." She picked up a yellow box of cigarettes from the porch and flipped its lid open. She removed one and lit it, then returned the box to the porch. "So, do you want to know what I think?"

"Obviously," Sam said.

"Okay." She paused before launching into it. "Sebastian Greely was a nobody, right? We talked about that. There aren't any books about him, but he was part of the art world for ages and befriended dozens of celebrated artists, so you find references to him here and there. Mostly in the biographies of his famous friends. He could shmooze them because he came from money. His family grew oranges in Florida. He was able to buy this place, not because he had a fortune from his own work, but because his stepfather was rich enough to fund his little vanity projects. Which, by the way, is a perfect throughline of the white elitist history of this place, from Kayo starting it as a spa for his rich white friends, all the way to Brandon and Fish.

"We know Greely and Florence were lovers. That's not in dispute. They were together in San Francisco, and it's documented that they were living together eighteen months later in New York. All the while, he had a wife and daughter back in Chicago, but they're not important to the story. That's just context. He praised her as his muse in letters to his famous friends in the art world. In some, he alludes to passing her around so they could benefit from her magical properties or whatever. But that might have just been a bad joke—you know, boys being boys."

"Gross," Sam said.

Roma nodded and exhaled a ribbon of smoke. "There's no direct evidence of Florence accompanying him to Indiana when he opened The Castle. The limited available information suggests they may have parted ways the previous year. So, to answer your question, that's why she's not tied to the official history of this property. There's a roster of people who attended the artist's retreat, and she's not anywhere on it."

"Okay," I said, "but why do you think she murdered him then? I mean, sure, he died, and someone buried the body, but he was an artist; isn't it more likely he overdosed or died from alcohol poisoning or suicide, and the artists just buried him to avoid a scandal?"

Again, Roma smiled. This time it was less of a showing-me-up kind of smile and more of a conspiratorial one, like we were all sharing some juicy gossip. "You're forgetting the cut marks on his bones. And anyway, like I said, Greely wasn't shit, so history has kind of cast him as a supporting character in other people's stories. But he knew people, including Jackson Pollock—he did those splatter paintings," she clarified, as if Sam and I didn't know. "Anyway, I visited the website for *The Archives of American Art* and found a letter Greely sent from this address to Pollock. It says something like, 'after a year of frustration, I'm finally rejoined with F.M., and my work has never been better.'"

"Florence Massey," Sam said.

"Bravo. And, by the few accounts we have, the work he accomplished with her was miles above his solo efforts. My theory is that Florence made that art, and Greely took the credit. The insult of being an unsung talent became too much for her, so she killed him and fled to Paris where the guilt drove her mad. Ergo the sanitarium and the 45 record to the throat."

"That happened a lot," Sam said, "men taking credit for the work of female artists. Rodin stole from Camille Claudel, Walter Keane stole from his wife. A bunch of other cases. But now Florence is back here as a ghost."

"Says you," Roma said. She stared into the distance as she finished the last of her cigarette. I glanced at Sam, who seemed lost in thought.

"Okay," I said, presenting the obvious question, "so, what do we do with this information?"

Without looking at us, Roma said, "I thought you'd never ask. Have either of you ever heard of a devil's mirror?

CHAPTER: 05

I.

To safely conjure the devil, Roma told us, you needed a church, a mirror, candles, a circle of salt, and the strength to keep your wits about you. We had everything but the church (and maybe the strength), but that was okay, probably, because it wasn't the devil we were conjuring. Sam said she'd watched about a million ghost hunting videos in her life and had never heard of anything like this. Roma said those videos were all clickbait trash, that her methods were the real deal. How did she know? She'd gotten super into the occult in high school and had read every book she could find on seances and conjuring. I asked, "Don't you need a psychic to do a conjuring?" Roma said there was no such thing as psychics, only scammers. Anyway, she said, we had something better. We had her, and she knew about the devil's mirror.

I'd be lying if I said I believed her. But I also wasn't entirely convinced she was just talking shit. That uncertainty was a big part of why I agreed to go along with her plan. I couldn't confess to the work I'd done with Florence because, despite everything, I didn't want that work to end. So, if Roma couldn't conjure her, no harm, no foul; we would continue secretly painting, and my openness to try The Devil's Mirror would show Sam I had nothing to hide. On the other hand, Florence had seriously scared me when she'd taken over my body. If we could get her to appear, maybe something we'd learn from her could reassure me she wasn't dangerous. It would be a huge comfort. In retrospect, it wasn't the smartest plan. I now know it did more harm than good, but I couldn't have known at the time. "So, when are we doing this?" I asked.

Roma stubbed out her cigarette then rose to her feet. "No time like the present, right?"

"Now?" Sam asked. She ran a hand over the front of her shirt, and I remembered how, beneath it, her stomach was cut up and bandaged and probably hurt like hell.

I nearly asked her if she could handle it or if we'd be better to wait, but then I glanced up at my bedroom window and thought of Florence pacing, waiting for me. "I think Roma's right," I said. "It's been a weird, emotional day, but maybe that's beneficial to the conjuring." I sounded like an asshole.

"I mean…if you guys want to, then I guess tonight's good with me."

"My hero," Roma said flatly.

"So, where are we doing this?" Sam asked, ignoring her snark.

"Your bedroom would be the best place," Roma said, "since you say you've seen her there."

"No. My dad."

"Fair." Her eyes rolled up to the sky as she thought. After a moment, she said, "The tennis courts, then."

"The tennis courts? Outside? At night?"

"That's where Sebastian Greely's body was buried. Assuming it was Florence who buried him there, the site will have significance to her. Now that I think of it, it was always the best place."

Even in the dark, I could see that Sam's eyes looked wide and frightened. I didn't like the idea of being out there any more than she did. At the same time, I was comforted by the thought of putting as much distance as possible between this ritual and my bedroom. "Okay," I said, "the tennis courts."

II.

We walked in darkness, lugging a vintage mirror from the common room and a reusable shopping bag which Roma had filled with candles and salt. I asked if they wanted me to grab some eye of newt or wool of bat to be safe, but neither of them thought I was funny.

The sky was overcast and barren of stars. Frogs chirped an endless round of song from the pond beyond the trees. We walked slowly over land we didn't know well even in daylight. I'd started to wonder if we'd gotten ourselves lost, but then Sam said, "There!" and led us to the tennis courts. We stood together on the broken clay, glancing at one another and then out into the darkness that surrounded us. "Now what?" Sam asked.

I would have expected there to be chanting or some kind of ritual involving slicing our hands open to consecrate the ground with our blood, but Roma just piled up enough sticks and rocks to prop up the mirror, spaced out the candles and emptied a canister of salt in an unbroken circle surrounding it all. She lit a cigarette followed by each of the candles and then took a seat, cross-legged, inside the circle. Sam and I stood back and watched her. She took five or six drags, then spat onto the clay and extinguished the cigarette with a hiss in the little puddle of spit. "Okay," she said, "we're ready." Sam and I each stepped into the salt circle. We sat facing the mirror on either side of Roma. She didn't acknowledge us, just kept her eyes on the mirror glass.

The silence became so overbearing I let out a nervous laugh. "So, should we join hands or something?"

"You wish," Roma said. "Keep laughing, and I'll join my hand to your face."

Sam said, "I think what he means is, how do we get started?"

"Dude," Roma said, "it isn't my ghost. I'm not even convinced there is a ghost. If you're ready, then start."

Sam looked to me for support, but I only shook my head, clueless. To Roma, she said, "I mean…I don't really know how to command her spirit to come to us."

"Just ask her to show herself. She's not a dog. You can't command her to do anything. Just invite her to come into the mirror."

In the flickering of the candlelight, I watched Sam take a steadying breath and close her eyes. She was sitting with her hands upturned on her knees in the common posture of meditation. I was surprised when I realized we all were. "Florence?" she called uncertainly. "Florence Massey? We—we would like to invite you to come and talk to us. We want to know why you appeared to me in my room and where you've gone since then. Do you need help of some kind? I'm inviting you to join us through this mirror." She opened her eyes. We were all staring down into the glass. It showed only the three of us, our faces distorted by candlelight, staring like idiot goblins. In her reflection, I saw Sam's eyes close again. "Do you know you're a ghost? You've passed over, but you can speak to us by coming into this mirror. If you come into this mirror, we can help you. We invite you to come and speak to us." Again, we waited. Again, no response came. Then, unexpectedly loud and forceful, Sam shouted, "I command the ghost that's haunting this property to show itself now!" The volume of her voice startled me, and a high-pitched squeal escaped my throat. Roma chortled, and after I got myself together, I smiled back at her, embarrassed, knowing I'd made a fool of myself. Sam's expression was serious, though. Her gaze stayed fixed on the mirror. "Look," she said, pointing.

The glass had begun to cloud. Our own reflections were still visible, but they were growing faint. It's hard to explain, but it wasn't exactly like we were being obscured by some mist or fog inside the glass. It was more like our reflections were being steadily erased and replaced with a scene from some hazy, neutral space. As we watched, a shadow began to form within that bland grayness. Slowly, it sharpened into a recognizable figure that was as clear as the three of us had been only moments before.

"Holy shit," Roma said.

I stared into the face of the white-haired man who was looking out at us. "That's Stanford Kayo," I said.

"Holy fucking shit," Roma said.

"Thank you," Sam said to Kayo, breathy, like a runner who's being interviewed immediately after a race. "Thank you for revealing yourself to us." Kayo's eyes slid in her direction. He was pale, and his face was pudgy above a collar and tie, but those eyes were uncanny. At first, I couldn't figure why. They were completely dry, I realized, dull and matte. Not a glint of moisture in them. They were the eyes of a dead man. "Mr. Kayo, does your spirit haunt these grounds?"

He opened his mouth slowly, like it took an effort to do so. In a voice that was high pitched and brittle like an old phonograph record, he said, "My wife."

"Your wife was Imogene Kayo," Sam said. "Is she with us too?"

The dead man squinted and repeated, "My wife."

"Do you want to go to your wife? Do you need our help to go into the light?"

It sounds crazy to say this about a dead man, but his expression grew cold at her suggestion. He didn't respond.

"Why are you stuck here?" Roma asked.

Kayo stared into the distance for long enough that I began to wonder if we'd lost contact with him. Eventually, though, he muttered, "Dalliances. Dalliances with the lamia. The dark rider." His face contorted into something pitiful. His words, which to me sounded like indecipherable nonsense, seemed to have caused him significant pain to say. None of us knew how to respond. He glanced at each of us, never blinking, having no need to moisten his dead eyes.

"Did you carve Sam's name into the door of the outbuilding?" I asked.

Sam looked at me, confused.

Kayo shook his head, once.

"Do you know the name, Florence Massey?" Roma asked. "Is Florence Massey with you?"

Kayo's forehead crinkled. He seemed to be puzzling over the meaning of those words, "Florence Massey." Abruptly, he cocked his head, looking past the frame of our mirror, seeming to be listening to sounds which only existed in the gray void he inhabited. Cautiously, he turned to look behind him, into the mist from which we'd conjured him.

I leaned toward the mirror, anticipating a reaction to whatever he was hearing. The others leaned in too. All at once, he looked back at us, his eyes wide, and he issued a feral scream that was so shocking I bolted backward out of the circle, a desperate act of survival which kept me from seeing the rainbow of colors Sam and Roma later swore entered the mirror, an array of light which seemed to attack him. What I saw, when I was able to register the mirror again, was blackness. Not supernatural, but an inky reflection of the real-life woods surrounding us. All our candles had gone out without my noticing. In the distance, the frogs had stopped chirping.

III.

I don't remember much about our march back from the tennis courts. I was numb and probably in shock. I think we all were. We barely spoke. Occasionally, one of us would curse in disbelief or begin to ask a question that would trail off and die in our throats. They made me carry the mirror, of course, which I held by its frame with my fingertips, the glass pointed safely away from me. In the empty common room, I shuddered at my own reflection as I returned it to its place on the wall.

Sam and Roma were waiting for me on the stairs. "Come on," Roma said, "we're going to mine." We didn't protest, just followed her up.

Roma's apartment was at the opposite end of the hallway from mine and Sam's. She unlocked the door and motioned for us to go inside. She'd just moved in that day, but the apartment had a mild woodsy smell which reminded me of gift shops I'd been in, years before, when we'd taken family vacations to the mountains. It gave me a surreal feeling, being in that space. I didn't belong in the private quarters of a college-aged girl. Despite the mound of unpacked luggage, I had the sense of being the only thing out of place in her living room.

Roma dropped the bag of used candles on the floor and fell back onto a ratty futon, which was the room's only furniture. "So, theories?"

"This place is haunted," Sam said after a pause.

"Good call. Sit down, both of you. You're making me nervous." She indicated a section of floor across from her. I sat and Sam did too, carefully.

I must have looked as uncomfortable as I felt because Roma asked me, "Are you losing your shit over there?"

"I mean, we did just conjure a ghost."

"That we did, but not the right ghost."

"I don't want to try again for the right one."

"No one suggested we should. But we need to use what we know to find out what we're dealing with."

"I have a theory now, I think," Sam said.

This piqued Roma's interest. "Okay, tell us."

Sam launched into it, the words coming quickly: "Well, I think they're being held here because they have unfinished business. Kayo and Florence, I mean. Maybe others, who knows?"

Roma rolled her eyes, which honestly seemed warranted to me in this case. The unfinished business thing was a cliché of every ghost story I'd ever heard. It wasn't much of a theory. "So, your hypothesis is that the ghosts haunting this place need us to help them with their unfinished business? And then, what? We feel all warm and fuzzy, and the ghosts pass over to the afterlife?"

Sam nodded.

"Like we're the Scooby Doo gang?"

"No, not like that."

Roma rested her head on the back of the futon and massaged her temples. "Well, the first problem with your theory is that Florence didn't die here; I told you that. Neither did Kayo. Florence died across the Atlantic Ocean, and Kayo died peacefully in his New York apartment. So, why would their spirits be trapped on these premises? If you believe in ghost mythology—and I'm not saying I do, necessarily—a spirit is supposed to haunt the place where it died."

"I was just trying to help," Sam said, clearly feeling scolded. "It was just a theory."

I agreed with Roma, but I was tired of her bluntness. "Kayo's wife, Imogene, died here," I offered, trying to help Sam out. "That's why he commissioned the statue out front. Greely died here too. Maybe Kayo and Florence are stuck on this property because this was where they were happiest."

"Yeah," Sam said, "like they died where they left their hearts." I thought this was a regrettable way of putting it.

"Aw," Roma said with mock sentimentality, "that's so gross." After a pause, she added, "I suppose we can't disprove hauntings work like that, though. So, for now let's put it in the *maybe* pile. There's another problem with your theory though."

"Of course, there is."

"It ignores the fact that Kayo mentioned a lamia."

"I don't know what that is," Sam said. I had never heard the word either.

"Well, unfortunately, we live in the only building in the United States of America that isn't wired for Internet, so I can't be sure either."

"But you can be sure Sam's theory is wrong?"

"I can't be sure of *exactly* what it is," Roma clarified, "but I know it's a mythological creature."

"How do you know that?" Sam asked.

She exhaled audibly, clearly reluctant to tell us. "Well, not that it matters, but I remember it from *Final Fantasy*."

"The video game?" I asked.

"Yes, the video game. Which I'm pretty sure Stanford Kayo never played, since he died a hundred years before it was released. It's based on real mythology, though. We just need to find out exactly what kind of creature it is."

We were all quiet then, annoyed with each other and clearly at a dead end.

Just when it seemed like this discussion was going to get us nowhere, Sam said, "My dad might know. He teaches religious studies. He has books about world religions."

"Well now," Roma said, a smirk raising one corner of her mouth, "look at you, being useful. Good call. Look through those books tomorrow. See if you can find anything." After a beat, she yawned deeply. "But…I'd say we need to call this meeting to a close for now. Unless someone has any other insights, I'd say we've gotten as far as we can tonight."

I was happy to get out of her apartment and readily shot to my feet. Sam raised her hand to me. I took it and helped her up, ignoring the nervous glance she gave me when I touched her skin. *Is this a monster touching me or just a stupid boy?* I gave her the kindest smile I could manage, but I knew a smile alone wouldn't settle her mind.

I walked ahead of her and opened the door. She was moving slowly. While I waited, I turned back to Roma in her futon and asked, "So what happens next?"

She acted like she hadn't heard me, kicking off her shoes and using each of her big toes to snake off the opposite foot's sock, making clear social time was over. "Next, you kiddies get a good night's sleep. I'm not sure after that. Don't worry, though, I'll have a plan by tomorrow. This is exactly the kind of shit I excel at."

IV.

It was nearly three o'clock in the morning, so I needed to be as quiet as the dead sneaking back to my room. With my shoes hooked on two fingers, I opened our apartment door just far enough to slide into the entryway. After easing it shut behind me, I padded to the hall in socked feet—where I promptly froze. The door to Jack's bedroom stood open. I wasn't religious, but I said a prayer asking that a late-night piss had gotten him out of bed, nothing more. Maybe, I should have rushed back to the living room to make it look like I'd slept on the couch. I should have at least gotten rid of my incriminating shoes. But, when his voice roared, "Get your ass in here, Milo!" I knew better than to hesitate. I came to his bedroom doorway, where I saw his silhouette sitting prone on the bed.

"Jack," I said with a put-on laugh, "you scared me." His bedside lamp clicked on. His expression was unreadable. "I…took a walk. I went to bed so early I woke up and couldn't get back to sleep."

"Were you with Sam?"

"No," I lied.

"I didn't hear Sam's door close just before you came in?"

"No."

"You weren't out in the moonlight with her, licking her wounds?"

"No, Jack. Of course not."

"Why is that easel set up in your bedroom? Have you been painting?"

"No, I was just…thinking about it."

"Mm-hmm." He dipped his head to one side then the other, and I heard the menacing crack of his neck from all the way out in the hall. When he spoke again, his words were slow and deliberate. "Do not think for one second, Milo, that I spent our inheritance to come and live in this bullshit community just to have you manipulate another troubled girl."

I hadn't realized how close I was to the edge, but this proved to be the final straw. The day had been too emotional, too big, too much. It had left me scared and tired. My eyes immediately brimmed with tears, spilled over, and brimmed again. "I never hurt anyone! *She* was picking on *me*! Rebecca and her friends bullied me ever since elementary school! I just wrote a dumb comment! I just did one dumb thing! How can you think I wanted any of this to happen? I hate this all so much, I hate—" But I couldn't say more. The words wouldn't come. I simply stood with my eyes locked on Jack's, my face snotty and tear-dampened, fully and pathetically on display for him. Judging from his expression, what he saw disgusted him.

After a moment, he cleared his throat. His arms were resting on his thighs, his fists opening and closing. "Trust is earned, Milo. Should I trust someone who sneaks out at night to do God-knows-what after I've gone to bed? *After* I told him to stay away from those girls...? No. I don't think so either." He raised his eyebrows, challenging me to speak, but I could only take deep, whimpering breaths, nothing more. "Go to bed, Milo," he said finally. "Stay there this time." I turned and started toward my room. "Milo!" I stopped. "Close my door. I have a work meeting in four hours." I did as I was told and headed down the hall.

My bedroom doorknob was cold to the touch. Ghosts were famous for making cold spots, I knew, sucking heat energy from an environment and using it to manifest. If I wasn't so scared Jack would murder me for disobeying him, I would have spun around and gotten as far from my room as possible. Instead, I turned the knob, feeling literal frost melt in my palm, then pushed the door open in one quick movement. I half expected Florence to be doing a paranormal show of temper in my room, levitating my bed or flinging canvases through the air. Everything seemed quiet, though. Cold and dark and quiet. I stepped in and hit the light. Nothing appeared to have been disturbed. "Hello?" I whispered, and I was able to see my breath, faintly. Even though I dreaded getting an answer, I called, "Florence?"

It was obvious she was present, and it was obvious she was angry. "That wasn't my idea down there," I said. "The conjuring, I mean. They were going to do it with or without me." I picked up a filbert paintbrush and nervously twirled its bristles into my palm. "Is he here too? Kayo? He seemed—agitated." I looked all around me, but no answer came.

I was exhausted, but I was also nervous to get into bed given the way she'd attacked me there earlier. We hadn't painted that evening. Maybe if I started a new canvas, it would calm her, put things right.

My palette from that afternoon still had usable oils, so I took it out of the drawer where I'd hidden it, grabbed an old canvas, and clamped it onto the easel. I dipped the filbert into a glob of navy-blue paint and started to apply it indiscriminately to the canvas, hoping she would guide me. I felt an immediate breeze against the back of my legs. I wanted to turn to look, but I kept working. When I ran out of navy-blue, I switched to burnt sienna, blending the two to create an amorphous, vaguely woman-shaped shadow. A rustling arose from behind me, accompanied by a pressure in the air that made my head feel like it might implode. I kept painting. To the navy and sienna woman-shape, I added ebony and orange, colors that were jarring to the eye and which didn't work together at all.

I continued even as the pressure built, and my heartbeat pounded in my temples. In time, I became aware of a steady, droning growl from a far corner of the room. The sound was visceral and unsettling. After several minutes of coaching myself to keep working, my distress finally overtook me. As casually as I could manage, I turned and looked. Florence had fully manifested. Her head was down, and I realized the awful sound was coming from the heavy rise and fall of her chest. Her hands were at her sides. She looked dangerous, and that look paralyzed me. It didn't occur to me to run, but I doubt I could have moved even if it had. Quietly, I called to her, "Florence?"

Her head snapped up. Her eyes locked on mine. The expression on her face was more vacant than angry. The impression it gave me was that I was witnessing a creature in the middle of some natural process which was intimate and not meant for me to see—like someone going to the bathroom or having sex. It wasn't good or bad, it wasn't right or wrong, it just was what it was. Slowly, she lifted her arms, spreading apart her thin fingers with her palms facing me.

"I'm sorry we did that with the mirror," I tried. "I didn't mean any harm."

At this, her growl turned into a scream. She rushed forward, and for the second time, I felt the pain of her entering me, of her fitting herself into spaces inside my body which were never meant to be filled.

V.

I blacked out, but it couldn't have been for more than a couple of minutes. I awoke in my bedroom, not far from where she'd attacked me. I was standing, or seemed to be, but I had no sense of my body— no feeling of balancing on my legs, no awareness of having weight or mass. Like when Florence took me to the hospital room, my own will was absent. In that case, though, I'd been consumed by Sam's thoughts and emotions. This time, I felt nothing. If Florence had an internal monologue like a living person, I wasn't in touch with it. Maybe she was blocking her thoughts from me. Or, I may have been experiencing exactly what it was like to be her—no feeling, just cold unemotional instinct.

It was only then I noticed my physical body lying crumpled at the base of my easel. My jaw was slack, and my eyes were only partially closed. Other than the faint sound of my breathing, I might have been a corpse. We turned and floated to my bed, then continued forward, passing through the bed and into the darkness of the wall separating my room from Jack's. We came out inside his room, turning to where he lay sleeping. He'd kicked off his blankets and was naked other than a pair of boxer shorts. We watched him for a long time, getting close to his face, listening to the wet rattle of his breathing. Our presence seemed to chill him, and he began to paw at his discarded blankets. We turned and moved on.

Roaming the second-floor hallway, we entered the bedroom of each of The Castle's residents. Roma slept in an oversized T-shirt with the logo of a band called *Dirty Pretty Things*, her legs and arms splayed in all directions on her air mattress. Fish and Brandon had an expensive-looking poster bed, and each slept on their sides, facing away from the other. The twins were both snorers and slept side by side on the lower mattress of a bunk bed. Dr. Rimini slept in a recliner in his office, his mouth wide open in an exaggerated yawn.

Lastly, we visited Sam's room. She lay on top of her covers, exposing the bandages on her arms and legs. She looked peaceful. Each time she inhaled she made a faint cooing sound from her throat. On the wall above her bed was the portrait that Florence and I had painted of her. We stood for ages, staring at it, until the nearness of us caused Sam to shiver in her bed, and we turned away.

After we'd visited every bedroom, we drifted down the curved staircase to the main floor, moving over every step but never touching them, before continuing out through The Castle's locked front doors.

We wandered the grounds in a snaking path with no apparent destination, startling raccoons and opossums and other night creatures, aware of them even when we couldn't see them with our eyes. Nearing the main road, we heard a sudden, high-pitched shriek echo from somewhere just beyond the border of the property. We changed course, moving toward the sound, stopping at the nearside of a drainage ditch which marked the property line. No vehicles were on the road in either direction. Far in the distance, a streetlamp shone a circle of light on the bare asphalt. Across the road from us, the trees were tall and thick.

Because I had no control, not even a body, I didn't jump or scream when a single great blue heron swooped down from a high branch and landed on the double yellow line in the center of the road. It stood opposite us, maybe ten feet away, posed with its long neck stretched up to bring it to its full height. Soon, a second heron landed beside the first, adopting this same posture. We raised our eyes to the treetops where we found the birds' roost just as a trio of them spread their wings and glided down to join the pair on the road. Five more followed. They stood side by side, wing to wing. In perfect unison, the ten herons swiveled their necks a fraction to the left, allowing each to train a single unblinking eye on us. They were an army in formation, still and silent, and, like an army, a promise of devastation accompanied their arrival. Whether they'd come to greet us or oppose us, I had no way to know.

We held like that until a pair of headlights appeared down the road to our right, coming this way. When the driver was near enough to slow and honk, the birds finally crouched and leaped into the air, one by one, to return to their nests. Once the driver passed, we turned, too, and headed back to The Castle.

I woke up on my bedroom floor, stiff and achy from the hours I'd lain on the hardwood. I couldn't explain the behavior of the herons, but I had no doubt about the point Florence had been trying to make to me—she was the owner of this property, and she was aware of everything that happened there. The Castle kept no secrets from her.

CHAPTER: 06

I.

I learned the next morning how creepy it feels to interact with people you've secretly watched sleeping. Jack had just left for his meeting, and I'd decided to take a walk to get my head around the craziness of the previous night. I hadn't made it much farther than Imogene Kayo's statue when a battered Nissan Altima roared up the driveway and came to a stop behind me. "Milo, get in!" a voice called.

I turned to see Roma sitting in the driver's seat looking as stern and impatient as ever. Sam's hand beckoned to me from the passenger window. I chose to approach them from Sam's side. "Hey."

"Jack's gone, right?" Sam asked.

I nodded.

"Then get in the back."

"What's going on?"

"We're going to the library," Roma said. "Let's go. You're coming with us."

The interior of the Altima smelled like stale cigarettes, an odor that was so sickening, I was grateful every time Roma lit a fresh one to mask it. Otherwise, it was surprisingly clean inside. "What about me made you think I was a slob?" she asked when I made some dumb comment along those lines. Her angry eyes met mine in the rearview mirror.

"Hey, look," I said, pointing at a passing farm, "cows."

It took us nearly thirty minutes to get into town from The Castle. I watched the land roll by, straining to see the big houses set far back in their yards. Hypnotized by the road, my mind wandered to thoughts of how I'd waited to get my temps until just before Mom and Dad's accident, but never even got a chance to practice in the car.

"Let me catch you up," Sam called back to me somewhere along the way. "I was telling Roma that Dad had a reference book with an entry on the lamia. She's a real creature from mythology."

"As I told you," Roma said smugly.

"Oh, yeah?" I asked, squirming a little in my seat. "So…what is it?"

"Well, that's the thing," Sam said, "it's not clear. Sometimes she's a vampire. Sometimes she's a half-serpent who eats children. Sometimes she's a demon. It changes culture to culture. She's never been one specific thing."

"Wrong," Roma said. "She's history's fear of powerful women. That's the one thing all the stories have in common."

I wasn't sure what to say. Florence was certainly powerful, and I was certainly becoming afraid of her. According to Roma, though, Florence had been a real person, not a creature from mythology. I didn't really get this line of investigation. "That's interesting," I said vaguely.

We fell into another silence. Eventually, a British voice from Roma's dashboard GPS told us our destination was on the right.

The Smithson Library was a steeple-roofed work of modern architecture—straight steel lines and rising panes of dark-tinted window glass. The parking lot was mostly empty, so we pulled into a space in the row nearest the building. Roma reached between the seats to grab a satchel from beside me, then we all stepped out into the hot afternoon sun. The broad walkway leading to the front doors was red cobblestone. Little trees had been planted in hollows on either side of it, leading from the parking lot to the building. We each took a minute or two to look around, ambling, before coming together into a group and walking to the glass front doors.

Inside, the air was cool and had the slight musty smell of all libraries. A long service counter ran along the wall to the left of the doors we'd come in through. Roma marched ahead of us, toward it. She dropped her bag on the counter in front of a thin, middle-aged man with a ponytail and round glasses. He was scanning books from a pile beside him and standing them one by one on a metal rolling cart. He looked up and smiled as Roma approached him.

Without offering him a greeting, she said, "We need to see the microfiche. Specifically, we need all local newspapers for two different periods: 1900 through 1910, and 1945 through 1965."

The man craned his neck back like he was blown away by her request. "Well, well," he said, widening his smile. "She knows what she wants, doesn't she?" He looked at me and winked. He had an awkward energy, like someone who'd learned about social interaction from a book with a title like, *How to Act Like a Regular Person.* "Is this for a school project?"

"I'm a journalist. It's for an article I'm working on. So, do you have what we're looking for?"

The librarian crossed his arms and tapped his chin with a boney index finger. "Well, yes, we have a newspaper archive on microfiche. I'm sure we have the *Indiana Republic* for those periods you're looking for."

"We'll want to see those too, but that's a statewide paper. What we want will be localized to this area."

His brow creased. His eyes began to sparkle at the deepening challenge. "I know for sure there isn't a regional paper covering this area now, but there may have been at one time. Let me check to see if there was ever—"

"There was. The *Post-Herald*. It was the local paper here from 1870 until it shut down in 1963. That's what we want. And the *Republic* too. Get those for us, and you'll also need to direct us to your microfiche scanner. While you grab all that, I'm going to run to the can. I need to pee." She lifted her satchel by its long purse strap and swung it toward Sam who caught it with both arms and hugged it against her chest, wincing from the pain it caused to her cuts and scratches. "Watch this for me," Roma said before disappearing down the narrow hallway where signs for the restroom were posted.

The librarian watched her go, then he turned to Sam and me like we could explain the hurricane that had just blown through his lobby. We gazed back at him, dumbly. After a few seconds, Sam cleared her throat. "Our microfiche?" she prompted.

When Roma returned, we were still waiting for him. Soon, he emerged through an open doorway behind his work counter. We heard him coming before we saw him, the whir of casters from the metal cart he'd piled up with a dozen or more plastic spools of film. "This way." He nodded toward some destination deeper inside the building.

We followed him past a glass-fronted snack area with a few tables and vending machines, around an expanse of computers providing Internet access to locals who needed it, and finally between two A-frame shelves of DVDs and Blu-rays. The library's collection of books was visible far to our right as if the contents of those shelves had been pushed aside by the snacks and movies and free broadband which appeared to be the building's main draw.

The librarian brought us to an area at the back of the building, a room walled by tinted glass panes with two clear glass doors. He stopped his cart in front of them. "Give me a hand?"

Sam and I moved to help him. Apparently, we both assumed Roma wasn't the type to open doors for others. Sam beat me to it, pulling one of the doors open by its brass handle. The librarian pushed his cart through. Roma entered, followed by Sam and then me.

The room was dimly lit compared to the library's main floor. Long, drawn sashes hung in the exterior windows, blocking out the natural light and leaving only two rows of fluorescent tube lights to illuminate the space. It appeared to be mostly used for storage. Tall shelves at either end of the room were filled with old-looking cardboard boxes. The focal point, however, was a table topped with two boxy pieces of electronics, each with its own small display screen. The units were the beige plastic of old-time personal computers like the ones Dad used to store in our garage. They were the microfiche scanners, I knew, even though I'd never seen one before. The table was furnished with a scattering of flimsy plastic chairs. The whole arrangement suggested that looking up old newspapers on microfiche was not the most common request made at the Smithson Library.

"Okay," the librarian said, lifting a spool of film from his cart, "there are some ground rules. You don't need to be supervised, but I do need you to be careful with this old equipment. Mostly, though, I need you to be respectful of these films. Each of these rolls represents the only copy of these documents we have in our archives. Microfiche is strong, so you shouldn't have any problems so long as you're careful. Sound good?" He didn't wait for an answer. "Okay, now let me show you how to load this film into the scanner..." He walked us through loading the plastic spool onto a spindle on the side of the machine and feeding the end of the film roll into its designated slot. Within seconds, a front page from the *County Post-Herald* displayed on the monitor. I'd never seen microfiche before, and I didn't realize it was just photographs of newspaper pages—every page of every paper photographed every day, day after day. I couldn't believe taking those pictures used to be somebody's job. The librarian showed us how to move the pages forward and back—a simple two-button command which caused a satisfying click when a page snapped into place—and how to rewind a spool once we'd gotten to the end of the film. "Got it?" he asked.

"Of course," Roma said.

The librarian seemed hesitant to leave, but soon enough he did. Roma pulled out a chair in front of the scanner he'd loaded. "Got it?" she asked Sam.

"Yeah, I think so." She took a seat at the other scanner.

There were only two, so I happily hung back.

"Good, look for anything to do with The Castle. Take your time. There may be something useful that's not an obvious front-page story. It might be deeper in the paper, and there may not be photographs. Keep an eye on the police blotters too." She turned to look at me. "Hey, bozo, don't just stand there." She motioned for me to sit in the chair in front of her. She moved out of my way. I came and sat. "The same goes for you. Keep your eyes open." After giving me this instruction, she headed toward the glass doors.

"Wait," Sam called, "where are you going?"

"You two have this covered. I'm going to see what I can find out from historical archives, documented oral histories from locals, that sort of thing. Don't worry about it. You have plenty to do here. I'll be done long before you will."

II.

Despite the effort of scanning through every film frame, we didn't learn much. Sam probably had the biggest score, finding a *Post-Herald* interview with Stanford Kayo from when he first broke ground on The Castle. He was already an obscenely wealthy man by then, and it was big news to the locals for someone of his stature to choose Indiana for his facility rather than New York or Chicago or wherever. He didn't mention the sins of masturbation in the article, but he used lots of coded words like 'purity' and 'moral health' and 'spiritual weakness.' We already knew he was a weirdo, though, so no surprise there. The important part was that he referenced his interest in pagan mythology, which was new information. He said pagan beliefs about spiritual fitness had been vilified by Christianity. He was a proponent of those beliefs and professed his disgust that their gods had been recast as demons by Christian conquerors. It must have been a pretty controversial position to take in the 1900s.

She showed the article to Roma, who followed up on it in the library's mythology section. Various pagan mythologies believed in a few different types of vampires. Some were the obvious bloodsuckers everyone naturally thinks of. Others were energy stealers, child stealers, body stealers—basically any kind of creature that gains strength from taking what's fundamentally yours and making it theirs.

I, uniquely, found nothing. I searched through those reels for hours, growing bored and anxious and wishing I was home. I kept my cool, but it got to the point where I was annoyed that they'd abducted me and stolen my day. I'd expected to paint that afternoon, to get right with Florence, and my separation from the work had begun to ache like a phantom limb.

We returned home around four in the afternoon. I didn't say much on the way back, but I managed to smile when we all parted ways.

III.

Florence rushed me the second I walked into my room. I didn't black out this time, which made me wonder if I was getting stronger as a host, or if she'd kept me awake to punish me. The pain was unbearable, a knife stab in every muscle she passed through. I felt an uncomfortable grinding as she slipped between my bones, into the miniscule cracks where they were fused. She was a scalding pressure that pushed out against my ribs and chests, and which rolled up my throat like fire. It only lasted seconds, but those seconds were miserable to endure. In the time it took my lungs to fill with the air I needed to scream, the pain ended, and that deep breath trickled out of my mouth as a long whimper.

In exorcism movies, the possessed person is always held hostage in their body, forced to watch helplessly as the demon attacks their family and vomits blasphemy at priests. In our case, I couldn't tell where Florence ended, and I began. A priest couldn't have coached me to use my own will to overpower her, because there was no difference in her will and mine. She controlled me, but that didn't mean I wasn't myself. I was just myself in a more significant form. Or, maybe, I'd become the spirit of Florence in a physical form. The point is, no clear division existed between us. Together, we possessed a talent as great as any master painter. I don't think I could describe the seductive power of making art that good.

We worked rough and fast like we were making up for my time away. We completed canvas after canvas. Five at least, maybe a few more. We painted with brushes and palette knives and the fingers of both my hands. They were new installments in the series we'd been working on. Renderings of faces made so close-up the features sometimes spanned multiple canvases—ears and cheeks, eyes that were closed and eyes that stared in unusual directions, mouths agape and mouths that appeared to be smiling. The work was grotesque and beautiful. We painted for hours, Florence's thin arm moving inside mine. When we were finally spent, we cleaned up and stashed each canvas under my bed. We'd completed so many by then they overlapped, the newer pieces likely smearing and smudging the older ones. We collapsed on my bed, feeling the eyes of those painted faces staring up at us as we rested.

We were awakened by a knock on my bedroom door, the sound of Sam's voice. Florence retreated—out of my body or deeper inside me, I wasn't sure. "Sam?" I called.

"Yeah, it's me."

She was in our apartment. Why was she in our apartment? I shot out of bed but hesitated to open my door. Sam, of all people, would recognize the odor of oil paint. My clothes reeked of it. "What are you doing in here?"

"I need to see you. Can you open the door please?"

I bared my teeth and cursed silently. Then I took a breath and cracked the door open. She was standing in the hall, only a foot from me. "You shouldn't be in here, Sam."

"Yeah, I'm sorry. I just—I was knocking and calling from out in the hall. I thought maybe something was wrong. It was unlocked." Her expression was pure apology until a flash of curiosity rippled across her face, and she asked, "Is that—oils?" She took a deep sniff of the air between us.

"You sound crazy right now, Sam," I said, narrowing the gap in the door. My words sounded harsher to me than I intended, or maybe I just immediately regretted how harsh I'd intended them to sound.

After a beat, she said, "You're probably right. I'm sorry. I'll go."

I should have let her, but the defeat on her face, that look of being hopelessly lost, was too upsetting. "No, wait. It's fine. It's just…what if I was walking around here in my underwear, you know?" She grimaced. "Go sit in the living room or something, and I'll be there in a second." I closed the door quickly before she could answer.

I changed into a clean shirt and shorts from my small closet then looked over my hands and arms for traces of paint. I hadn't gotten my nails completely clean, but I could hide them in my lap or in balled fists. I went to join her in the living room, closing my bedroom door behind me.

"So, what's up?" I asked, taking a seat opposite her on the couch, as far away as I could get.

When she spoke, her words sounded tentative. "I don't know. It isn't really anything. I just wanted to talk to you. It probably wasn't worth barging in."

"You're fine," I said, only half meaning it. I stopped my leg from its nervous bouncing, then turned toward her deliberately, opening myself up to her like I had nothing to hide. "What did you want to talk about?"

"God, I don't know…" she moaned, breaking down, my simple question having opened the floodgates. She sat forward and held her face in her palms, rocking forward and back. "It's just all so much, you know? The lamia. Stories that she's a demon or a vampire? When we got home, I laid in bed and started reading through Dad's book again, and I guess I just kind of creeped myself out."

I lowered the volume of my voice hoping to sound kind and consoling. "Sam," I said, "you don't really think this place is haunted by a vampire demon? Or wait—would it be the ghost of a vampire demon?"

She raised her head and turned to me. Her cheeks were slick with tears. A few strands of hair fell across her face. She had a single strawberry-shaped freckle on the end of her nose. I'd noticed it before, but I felt something stir inside me as I gazed at it now. "No, of course not," she said. "Vampires aren't real. I don't know about demons, but we know Florence Massey was just a regular person. I guess I don't know what to think… But she came to me, you know? She was after me. What did she want from me, Milo? I've been laying in my room wondering what you saved me from by scaring her away that day."

Hearing her say that name, Florence Massey, set my body tingling. The sensation was odd and nearly overpowering, like I was being drawn to the sweetness of those words on her lips. I'd heard her say the name a dozen times, and I'd never had that reaction. I smiled like nothing was wrong, even though I strongly suspected something was. Sam smiled back. Her eyes looked puffy. She was so close to me, so vulnerable. That vulnerability, I realized, was filling me with a growing desire to do…*something*. Something alarming. Something that would amount to stealing from her, taking advantage. In what way, I wasn't sure. Horrified, I bolted off the couch and crossed the room. "Don't worry about it," I managed to say, though my throat suddenly felt constricted. "She's stopped bothering you now, and that's all that matters."

"Milo, are you okay? You're acting—"

"Look, Sam, Jack could come home any minute. He wouldn't like it if he found you here."

"Oh, okay. Yeah, sure. Sorry. Are you okay, though?"

"Of course. I'm great."

She stood, remaining at a distance from me, her brow creased as she sized me up, worrying one of the bandages on her arm. "Really, I guess I just wanted to say thank you."

"Yeah, no problem."

"Right…cool. I'll see you at dinner then, I guess."

"Right. I'll see you." I turned my back to her and stayed that way until I heard the front door latch. Once she was gone, I opened the living room window for air and stared across the grounds for a long time. I felt like a monster, unsure whether it had been me with Sam just then or if it had been Florence.

IV.

At dinner, Fish suggested tonight should be the first of a weekly all-resident board game night. "We can have competitions, tiered play. Perhaps even prizes." The twins were all for it, clasping their hands and bobbing up and down in their chairs. Dr. Rimini said he was in, which meant Sam was, too, by default. Roma rolled her eyes, of course. "Jack? Milo?" Fish asked.

"Yeah, I don't know," Jack said. "I mean, not tonight, probably, but I can play sometimes, maybe."

"Milo? Are you less of a humbug than your brother?"

Jack shot me his usual judgmental glare. Rather than cowering, though, or moping, I stared right back at him. It didn't even occur to me to look away. "Actually," I said, "Jack doesn't hate board games, it's just the idea of being in my presence for so long that freaks him out. See, look at him. I make his skin crawl just sitting across the table from him." As I heard these words come out of my mouth, a wave of warmth washed over my face. It was all true, but I never would have thought to confront him about it, even if it were just him and me, let alone in front of other people. I never would have, and yet I did.

"Oh, that's not true," Fish said, "Jack looks perfectly—well, no, he does look a little miffed, I suppose. But I'm sure it's only because you'd suggest something so unpleasant about him." He was right about Jack looking miffed. His face was as red as a burning coal.

Horrifyingly, I pushed further: "Is that right, Jack? Are you upset because I can't see how much you love me? How I don't appreciate that everything you do is for me? Do you want to hang out with me tonight and play games and have some quality time together, Big Brother?" I felt like I could throw up. Jack's jaw was clenched and flexing.

"Shit," Roma said. "If this is what game night is going to be like, count me in."

Jack was staring at me like he might reach across the table and wring my neck. "Sure, Fish," he said, "I'll play."

"Well, then…good," Brandon said with an uncomfortable smile, "then we're all on board. Won't this be fun?"

V.

Game night is mostly a blur to me now. That instinct to harm—first Sam in the apartment, and then Jack at dinner—subsided. Something was still wrong inside me, though, and it was hard for me to focus on anything else.

I ended up in a game of Monopoly with Sam, Jack, Fish and Roma. The others broke off into a second group to play something more age appropriate for the twins. I required repeated reminders when it was my turn, when I had to roll the dice or pay someone money. I quickly lost, then watched the others play from what felt like a great distance away. Roma was a vicious silver thimble who systematically bankrupted us one by one—first me, of course, followed by Sam and then Jack. I remember Sam staring at me with a worried look on her face after she was out. Even Jack looked concerned. "Mano a mano," I remember Fish saying when it was just the two of them.

Roma stared across the board at him. "You have no chance of winning."

"Well, I haven't lost yet," Fish said, taking up the dice, "so statistically, I do have a chance."

"Statistically, you're a dead man walking. Not the first murder this place has seen, either."

This comment focused my attention. Or something inside me focused. *Florence?* I remember calling to her in my mind, hoping for confirmation that these strange feelings were just her still inside of me. I considered the possibility, too, that she'd broken my body and mind. Either way, I received no response.

Fish took his time moving his silver Scottie dog around the board as if, in delaying, he might change the fate of his roll. "Murder seems a little dramatic for game night, don't you think?"

Roma watched his fingers with a glint in her eyes. She'd counted ahead and knew the trap of hotels he was headed toward. "No," she said, "but if you want drama, we can talk about The Castle ghosts."

"Ghosts again?" he asked. His fingers hovered over the board. He landed the silver dog in its final resting place hard enough to rattle every house and hotel on the board. He took up the few remaining bills in his bankroll and began to count out what he owed. "I'm a spiritual man, Roma. But more along the lines of chi."

"Don't give me your hippie nonsense," Roma said. "You've lived here longer than any of us. You're saying you've never even suspected there are ghosts?"

"Milo?" Sam whispered. A fluttering had begun in my chest, and it started my body shivering.

Fish persisted, oblivious to me. "The Castle has atmosphere, a palpable history, that's all. *Ghost* is an ignorant characterization."

"Fine. Call them whatever you want—ghost, phantom, wraith, duppy, specter. They're here, whatever you call them. Last night, we summoned the spirit of Stanford Kayo."

I wanted to tell her to stop talking about this, but I couldn't talk myself. A mild electric shock had started in my feet and arms. It spread up the sides of my face. I was doing all I could not to draw attention to it.

"Stanford Kayo?" Fish said with a hearty laugh. "Isn't that nice? Brandon! We're being haunted by Stanford Kayo!"

"Oh, fun," I heard Brandon say.

"Listen," Fish said, returning his attention to Roma, "next time you talk to him, tell him I wasn't a fan of those limited pumpkin spice Corn

Nibs last Fall. They left a sort of film on the palate." He tossed all his bills into the center of the board. "You win, by the way."

"Laugh it up. It doesn't make it untrue. There's something darker here too…"

My ears began to ring, and I lost the rest of their words. I watched Roma flagrantly talk about Florence and the lamia. As I did, I felt the full force of Florence's anger at being discussed this way. The feeling left no doubt that she was still somewhere inside me.

My memory tells me Fish went pale.

My memory tells me the room went cold.

All at once, I screamed—a wailing so loud I heard it myself, even though my ears had temporarily gone deaf. I remember Sam beside me, holding my arms, Jack on his feet above me. My head pushed back against the couch's seat cushions. My eyes rolled up into my skull. My body shook and seized. My throat formed primal sounds—gurgles and moans like a rabbit caught in a trap, desperate sounds like the great blue heron made when its leg was caught in the fishing line. Eventually, Florence showed me mercy and allowed me to black out. I wouldn't wake up from that sleep for what felt like a very long time.

CHAPTER: 07

I.

We stood over the body in the hospital bed with its oxygen tube and its taped eyes. It belonged to both of us now. Trauma had been done to it when we'd fused, and it responded to the shock by shutting down. The coma was shallow, but the doctors couldn't say how long it would last. They were still running tests. Jack sat in a chair beside the bed, scrolling on his phone.

II.

While our body slept, our consciousness roamed The Castle. Even from miles away, in a hospital in a neighboring county, every thought, every action, every word spoken on the property remained available to us. The effort of watching was exhausting, though, so we limited our gaze to Sam and Roma, the two who would attempt to stop us.

Hours earlier, the EMTs had arrived at The Castle to stabilize us, bringing chaos to the common room. Sam had looked on, hugging her father around his middle like a little girl. She'd once witnessed a similar scene with her mother. For the endless minutes they'd worked on us, she'd unknowingly clenched a plastic Monopoly house in her fist.

After the ambulance drove us away, she curled into herself on the common room's couch. A memory had gotten stuck in her mind—her ninth birthday when her mom and dad had taken her to see *The Phantom of The Opera*. They'd been robbed in the parking garage after the show. They had just gotten back into the car when her mom's door was pulled open and the world was suddenly filled with a man's echoing shouts and the menace of a gun, demands for money. Her parents did exactly as the man said. They handed over their cash, and her mom didn't fight when he snapped the necklace from her throat.

Sam had been small and terrified then, but as she remembered it, those seconds spanned an eternity. Afterward, when it was just the three of them in the car, the stillness was oppressive. She imagined her mom and dad wanting to scream and run after the man, fight him even, but the stillness held them in place like a second assault. Sam wanted to wail and beat her fists against the car window, but all she could do was sit in the backseat with her hands folded in her lap while her dad gripped the steering wheel, and her mom cradled her empty purse. She remembered feeling paralyzed. The common room was like that for her, too, after they took our body away. There had been so much confusion when the EMTs rushed in, leaving the residents breathless and awkward in the corners of the room. None of them had known what to do, just like in those first moments in the car after they were robbed at *The Phantom of the Opera*.

Soon, Brandon ushered the twins upstairs, Fish at his elbow, the two of them frantically whispering. Roma offered a single, dry declaration of, "Jesus Christ," then moved toward the exterior doors with an unlit cigarette already wobbling between her lips.

When they were alone, Dr. Rimini asked Sam, "Honey, did Milo ever mention being epileptic?"

"No. He never said anything like that."

He nodded into the distance. "Well, I don't know about you, but I think I've had just about enough of ambulances for one week."

"Me too."

He sat on the couch beside her. He, too, was thinking about his lost wife. We felt the strength of their bond through their shared grief. "So,

Roma's pretty cutthroat at Monopoly." His attempt to lighten the mood.

Sam gave him a weak smile. "Are you surprised?"

"I couldn't say. I've never really spoken to her. Not at any length. But I've never been so frightened of a thimble before, I can tell you. Is she so intense when you hang out together?"

"I mean, yeah, pretty much. I think intense is kind of her default. It's good, though. Roma's good. I like her."

"Well, honey, I think that's great. I'm glad you're making friends." He touched her hair with the back of his fingers. "I think, though, it might be a good idea for you to turn in early tonight. This evening was pretty upsetting, and you're still not one hundred percent."

Sam stared at the outer doors. She needed to talk to Roma, but she really was exhausted. "Okay," she agreed. "Bed sounds pretty good, actually."

"I think it's best. Should we clean up first?" He rose to his feet with a performative groan then motioned to indicate the game boards, plastic pieces and fake money which were strewn all around.

"No. Let's leave it."

"Good girl." He led her toward the stairs. "Let Fish and Brandon do it. The elites cleaning up after the working person for a change."

We traveled with them up the grand staircase and down the second-floor hallway. Dr. Rimini struggled to think of something more to say to console her, and we felt his frustration when nothing came to him. Inside their apartment, he asked, "Do you want to talk more about anything?"

"No, thank you, Dad."

"Okay." The ends of his moustache turned up a little when he smiled. "Do you want a snack? I have Newtons in my office."

"I'm okay. I'm just going to go to bed."

"Sounds good. I just—I'm here. If you need me."

"I know, Daddy. I'm here too."

The emotion in his throat came out as a single pulse of laughter. "Thanks, kid," he managed. "And I know where to find you should I need you—one door down from mine. Goodnight, honey."

After he'd closed himself in his office, Sam filled a coffee mug with water in their tiny kitchen nook then leaned against the counter, imagining us in our hospital bed, awake and healing. Thoughts of the hospital made her skin itch under her bandages. From down the hall came the sound of her father gently padding across the hardwood floor and closing the bathroom door. Only a second later, it squeaked back open. Curious, she stopped what she was doing and listened. She nearly dropped her mug when the door abruptly slammed shut again.

"Dad?" she called.

She was halfway down the hall, standing in front of the closed bathroom door, when Dr. Rimini stepped out of his office. "Sam? Are you all right?"

She could only blink at him in response.

They locked eyes, confused. Dr. Rimini began to speak, but before he could, a rapid succession of bangs sounded from inside the bathroom. "Sam!" He pulled her toward him. She broke free easily and placed a tentative hand on the bathroom doorknob. He reached but fell short of stopping her.

The room was dark. Dr. Rimini stepped up just behind her, his chest pressed against her shoulder. They craned their necks and listened. The hollow tap of old plumbing echoed from the bathtub. Otherwise, everything was quiet.

After a beat, Sam reached through the doorway and slid her fingers along the wall, searching for the light switch. Once she'd found the panel, she hesitated, then flipped the switch on.

Nothing was out of place. Just their ordinary, tiny bathroom.

She took one step forward, then another. Her hands were extended, her fingers spread wide, as if she expected to feel a cold spot or some sort of energy field. Dr. Rimini hovered in the doorway, too afraid to go further. Quietly, Sam called, "Florence?" We ached at that call, at that name on her lips.

All at once, the mirrored door to the medicine cabinet began to flutter violently, opening as far as its hinges allowed before flinging shut, opening and closing, again and again. Sam leaped back against the wall opposite the sink, taking the blunt edge of a towel rack to her shoulder.

"Sam!" Dr. Rimini shouted, but he stayed fixed in the doorway.

Each time the cabinet door sprung opened, items dropped from the shelves into the sink basin—pill bottles, Sam's hairbrush, a toothpaste tube, bobby pins. She was readying herself to run past the mirror, back to the safety of the hall, when the activity abruptly stopped. The cabinet door quieted, creaking forward only from inertia until it stilled completed.

Sam looked all around her for where it would move next—raising and lowering the toilet seat, maybe, or turning the shower head on and off. We felt the steady thrum of her heartbeat.

"Sam, come out of there, honey. Come out of the bathroom."

She nodded, but before she could run to him, the medicine cabinet door slammed shut for a final time, cracking the glass and causing them both to cry out. Sam saw herself framed in the broken mirror's reflection—her wide-eyed stare, her figure pressed against the wall. While she watched, the glass began to fog as if from the steam of a hot shower, overlaying her reflection with that of another. "Kayo," she gasped. At the sight of him, Dr. Rimini shot back reflexively, thudding against the wall on the opposite side of the hallway. We watched, irate. With our body so many miles from The Castle, we were limited in the ways we could stop him.

Kayo's eyes were wild with delight. A mischievous smile contorted his lips. He stared, unblinking, at Sam. "The lamia," he said in his strange, high-pitched voice, "has left these grounds!" His tittering laugh was like the squeak of a rusty bicycle wheel. His smirk bloomed into a full, broad grin. "She has gone. For the first time in more than a century, she has gone. How did you—" he began, but then stopped. We had focused ourselves in the narrow space between Sam and the mirror, directing our rage at him. Sensing us, his expression changed from euphoric to quizzical. He cocked his head, feeling us near him but struggling to understand just where we were. When he finally found us, he winced. "You did not send it away?" he demanded.

Sam shook her head. "No."

"I thought…I might have sworn you…"

"I didn't do anything at all. But she took my friend."

"Yes." Kayo lowered his head. "Yes, I see you did nothing. The lamia has left these grounds. But it watches still. And it will return, stronger in its host. It will return with the strength to kill you all."

Sam said nothing, just stared into the mirror with an expression that was dumb and disbelieving. Kayo averted his eyes like he was too disgusted to look at her.

It was tiring for us to demonstrate so much anger, and we began to fade. We were only dimly aware of Kayo blinking off. Faintly, we heard Sam crying, felt Dr. Rimini coming to her, calling her name. We saw her reach for him and collapse into his arms.

Exhausted, we pulled our awareness back from The Castle.

III.

While we slept, Florence showed me moments from her life, how she was born to Irish immigrants in a slum in New York at a time when Irish Americans were treated as second-class citizens. I recalled every assault against her—the slaps from her stern father, the lumps of coal and sod thrown at her by her classmates, the more troubling encounters with local men when she was growing into womanhood—as if they were my own memories.

She was a spirited child whose confidence couldn't be bullied out of her with violent hands or sticks or clucking tongues. From a young age, she was told by her mother that the best she could hope for her life was to become a seamstress or a nanny for one of the few rich families that wasn't afraid to bring Irish blood into their home.

Florence wouldn't have it.

At an early age, her interest in art was sparked by the images on her father's matchbook covers. She would sneak them out of the wastebasket and hide them in a slit she'd ripped in her straw mattress. She fabricated her first paintbrushes by snipping tufts of stiff hair from the mongrel dogs that haunted the streets of her neighborhood and affixing them to whittled sticks. I could feel the ghosts of those brushes in my hand. I felt the stinging bites on my face and arms when the dogs objected. She made her own paints from soot and chickweed and dandelions plucked from sidewalk cracks, mixing them with discarded cooking oils to form sludgy pastes which left her early art stinking of animal fat. I saw the prodigious quality of her work, even with her low-quality materials, on her early canvases of rotted wooden floorboards and shards of broken bricks. I felt the terror of being a young girl searching alone through ghetto alleys for these materials.

At the age of fourteen, Florence left home for good. I heard the rage of her father's drunken screaming, his baseless accusations that she wasn't pure or chaste, that she was a trifling whore. I jumped at the shattering sound of a thrown whiskey bottle. I felt the heartrending tug of regret as she ran from their tenement room, ignoring the pleas of her mother for her to come back.

She showed me happier times, too, memories from years later. They were like reels of film unspooling in a dark corner of our mind. They unspooled even as we regained enough strength to return our attention to The Castle.

IV.

"I would like you to tell me what's going on here. Right now, please." Dr. Rimini was saying. He and Sam were in the dining hall, where they'd found Fish and Brandon sitting at a table with a ledger open between them. Sam and Dr. Rimini were standing.

"I'm not sure what happened in your apartment," Brandon said, "but I'm certain it was nothing supernatural." The aura of pleasant goodwill which both men typically projected was noticeably absent. Still, they didn't seem rude as much as exhausted.

"I *told* you what happened in our apartment," Dr. Rimini said.

"So, you did. And do you want me to tell you what I think? I think we had a very upsetting night. We're all worried about Milo. I think you had a minor breakdown. Which, of course, is completely understandable given the circumstances."

"I didn't have a breakdown," Dr. Rimini insisted. "Sam saw it too."

Brandon glanced at Sam and then back to Dr. Rimini. "Fine. Let's say you saw a ghost, then. Even if that's the case, there's no more information I can give you."

"It was Stanford Kayo," Sam said.

Brandon continued like she hadn't spoken. "We're not aware of any reports of paranormal activity in the property's history. Personally, I don't even believe in ghosts. I'm not sure what else you want me to say."

We felt Dr. Rimini's uncertainty in how to respond. He didn't know what he wanted from them either; he only knew something needed to be done. "I think," he began but paused when no specific demand came to him. In the end, he settled on, "I think we should change apartments."

"Change to a less haunted one, you mean?" Fish asked. "Dr. Rimini, as Brandon pointed out, it's been a trying night for us all. A trying week, if we include what happened to Sam. But it will do no one any good if we start giving in to fanciful thinking. I mean, Stanford Kayo? I'm not qualified to say one way or the other if you and Sam experienced some shared delusion, but it's obvious where the suggestion for your ghost came from. Do you recall Roma mentioned Stanford Kayo only moments before Milo's medical episode?"

"Oh, sure," a voice echoed from the direction of the kitchen, "blame it on me." They all turned to see Roma, who was walking toward them, her heels tacking on the floor with each step.

"Roma, have you been spying on us?" Fish demanded.

"Spying?" She gave a short, barking laugh. "I wasn't spying on anybody. I just got hungry and wanted to see if there was more of

Brandon's delicious mutton. And then you all showed up, and I didn't want to interrupt. You invoked me, though, so here I am."

"It wasn't mutton," Brandon said, "it was lamb."

"Is there a difference?"

"How much did you hear?" Fish asked.

"I heard my name. Did you say anything else of importance?"

"No, The Riminis were just lodging a complaint about a pest in their bathroom."

"Fish!" Brandon scolded.

"Gross," Roma said. She turned her attention to Sam. "If you saw one, though, that means there's more. That's the thing about vermin."

"It was surely only the pipes rattling," Brandon said. "Now, if you could go, please, Roma, we can finish up here."

"Fine. I hope they aren't in my apartment too. Sam, do you want to come look with me?"

"Dad?" Sam asked, but Roma was already tugging her toward the hall.

They were silent as Sam followed her up the stairs. When they reached the second-floor landing, Roma turned to her and asked, "So, what happened?"

Sam told her about the activity in their bathroom mirror, how Kayo said when we returned, we would be strong enough to kill. We felt a shiver run through Sam's body as she recalled his words. She stood expectantly, waiting for Roma's reaction.

"Your dad heard?"

"I mean, yeah, he was standing right there. He heard everything."

"So, does he believe you about what we've found out?"

"It didn't come up. Between our bathroom attacking me and Kayo's threat that Milo wants to murder us, I was a little distracted."

"Good." Roma turned to the right and headed down the hall.

"Roma?" Sam called.

She stopped.

"I thought we were going to *your* apartment." She extended a finger in the opposite direction.

"Let's go to yours instead." Without waiting for permission, she started down the hall.

Sam jogged to catch up with her. "Okay, I guess that's fine." She moved ahead of Roma to unlock the door then peered over her shoulder. "But, I mean, why, exactly, are we going to ours? My dad will probably be back any minute. He wasn't really getting anywhere down there."

"That won't be a problem." She placed her hand over Sam's on the doorknob and guided her to push the door open. "Hey, it looks just like mine." she said, appraising the apartment from the entryway. "Nice mini fridge. Your bedroom's this way?" She moved down the hall.

Sam stood, watching her. In the preceding hours, she had seen us go into a violent seizure and was then informed by a deceased breakfast mogul that she would be murdered by an oil-painting pagan vampire wearing the skin of her friend. Now, she had this to deal with, whatever this was. It seemed there would be no end to the strangeness of this day.

Roma came to Dr. Rimini's office, opening the door and glancing over the stacks of books and the old-fashioned word processor, before pulling it shut again and moving across the hall to the bathroom. "It happened in here?"

Sam nodded.

Roma flipped on the light and peered in. Nothing unusual caught her attention, so she continued down the hall. At Sam's door, she glanced back before turning the knob and disappearing inside.

"Hey," Sam called, hurrying along behind her, "what are we doing again?"

When she got to the doorway, she found Roma standing beside her bed, transfixed by our portrait of her. Sam waited, realizing she had never shown Roma the extraordinary quality of our work. She gave her time to sit with it. While she waited, she glanced around her room, seeing it through a stranger's eyes—her unmade bed, the clothes (blessedly not underwear) strewn here and there, the paint supplies which were literally everywhere. Eventually, Roma turned to her. Her eyes showed an unfamiliar depth of emotion. "This painting makes you look so sad, but also really beautiful."

Sam could only nod her agreement.

After taking a final moment with the portrait, Roma lowered her eyes and forced herself away from the bed, moving between Sam and the pair of easels which still stood back-to-back on her rug. She came to the window and stared out into the night. "Does this open?"

"I assume. I've never tried."

Roma took the window latch between her fingers and pulled. When it didn't budge, she adjusted her grip and pulled it with both hands.

Sam stood back, watching her struggle and fail. "Okay, I'm going to need you to tell me what's happening here."

"Tell you what, exactly?" Her voice was strained from exertion.

"Why are we in my room? Why are you at my window? What is it we're doing?"

Roma turned away from the window and furrowed her brow. "Why? Are you uncomfortable with me being in here?"

"No, I just—I'm tired of you keeping things from me like I'm a child. You need my help as much as I need yours."

Roma nodded. "Surprisingly, that's true. Do you have a knife or something? There's paint sealing this window closed."

Reluctantly, Sam went to her desk and grabbed a palette knife from her painting supplies. "You can't smoke in here, if that's what you're thinking. My dad will smell it even if you do it out the window. Anyway, I don't like it."

Roma took the knife and began to run it around the perimeter of the latch and along the edges of the window. "I had a smoke outside just before I came and got you. That's what gave me the idea."

"The idea for what?" Judging from the sound of Roma's aggressive sawing, she imagined this would be the end of her palette knife's usefulness.

"I was walking the grounds," she explained as she worked, "having a cigarette and looking up at the building." She reached behind her and returned the bent knife to Sam. "I noticed your apartment was right beside Milo's."

"You already knew that."

"Yeah," she said like this was a ridiculous observation, "but why would it have mattered to me before now?"

"That's what I'm trying to figure out!" Sam cried. "Why does it matter to you?"

Roma succeeded in unhooking the latch then pressed the heels of her palms against the upper rail of the window. She planted her feet in a broad stance, using her entire body to push as she tried to muscle the window open. "What I noticed looking up at the building tonight," she groaned, "was Milo and Jack left one of their apartment windows open." At this revelation, Sam's own window popped and slid two-thirds of the way up. Roma exhaled, proud, then clasped the window from the bottom and forced it the rest of the way up. She turned to Sam with satisfaction, wiping her hands on her pant legs. "I figure, since they'll probably be gone all night, we can take this opportunity to have a look at what Milo's been hiding from us."

Sam's first reaction was to laugh. When Roma's expression didn't change, she was horrified by the realization that she was serious. "Are you crazy?" she demanded.

"That's been the opinion of some. But you can't deny what happened to him tonight, Sam. We all watched her take him. Kayo confirmed it in your mirror. Florence is inside Milo. So, I'm just wondering how long she's been grooming him."

"Grooming?"

"Of course. Think about it. Why would she do it tonight in front of everyone? It's because I was bringing everything out into the open to Fish. So why, then, would she take Milo? Why not me? I was the one running my mouth. Or you, even? You're Kayo's favorite, apparently. She's gotten stronger since you last saw her in your bedroom, and that didn't happen without someone's help."

"And you think Milo…"

Roma's tone was gentle when she said, "I'm sorry to say it, but yeah, I think Milo. He's been communing with her this whole time, opening himself up to her. Just like you suspected when she stopped coming to you. I think you were right all along, Sam."

We felt her heartache when she accepted the truth that we'd been lying to her. She had a flash memory of watching our videos in her hospital room. She hadn't been sure that night, after reading about Rebecca Steiner, if Milo Selby was a mixed-up kid or a predator. She didn't like which option our lying suggested. "Okay, fine," she said, shaking her sadness away, "but, I mean, you want to break in? You really want to shimmy across the ledge and break into his room?"

"We don't need to shimmy. The ledge is super wide." Roma pushed her head and shoulders through the window to confirm its width. "Jesus Christ!" she shouted, leaping back into the room.

"What? What is it? Is it Milo?"

Roma was doubled over, breathing heavily with a hand over her heart. She shook her head and smiled. Her heavy breathing became a short, ironic laugh. "No. It's one of those damned herons. It's on the ledge between the apartments."

Sam made a quizzical face and hurried to the window. She hesitated before peeking out. There, on the ledge, just as Roma said, was a single great blue heron. It was three feet from her, maybe less. Its nearness sent a sympathetic ache through her healing body. "Hi," she said to it reflexively, her voice breathy and faint. The heron tilted its head as it considered her, like it was sizing up the tastiness of a vulnerable fish. Just for a moment, their eyes met. Then, it unfurled its wings and leaped into the night, vanishing from her sight.

"No," Sam said, coming away from the window. "We shouldn't do this. That was an omen."

"It was a bird," Roma corrected. "This place is lousy with them. They're everywhere." She returned to the window and confirmed that the heron was gone. "Cool, let's go."

Sam shook her head. "I don't think we should. Actually—I'm sure I can't."

"Well, I guess it's up to you. But personally, I don't plan to get murdered by a lamia. You can stay here to be a lookout if you want to pretend to be helpful. Just bang on the wall or something if you happen to see their car come up the driveway."

"Wait!" Sam half whined the word, half crying it. She sounded pathetic even to herself.

Roma took one last glance at her before stepping onto the ledge.

V.

Everything changed for Florence in San Francisco. After running away from home, she spent five years traveling the United States, searching for a community that would accept her. She developed into an outstanding oil painter. Nevertheless, it was hard for her to break into the male-dominated art world, so she often supported herself by tending bar or doing strenuous, low-paid factory work. She became romantically involved with several male artists, relationships which were sometimes founded on genuine affection but were mostly strategic partnerships.

One of these relationships, a brief and passionate affair with a Seattle photographer, brought Florence to the attention of the middle-aged San Francisco sculptor, Jamison James. James had once been a wildly successful artist. In his long career, a dozen of his pieces had been commissioned by national parks and installed in government buildings across the western United States. At the time Florence knew him, however, he was suffering from an artistic block and steadily failing eyesight, and he was on the market for an in-shop assistant. Florence had never sculpted previously, but she was charming and pretty and talented enough to become an asset to him once her charisma got her in the door.

In her four years at his shop, James experienced a professional renaissance. No one knew that his late work was entirely based on models carved by his young protégée, that his designs owed their quality to the creative mind of Florence Massey. James compensated her well, though. Through her association with him, she quietly honed her talents to those of a master. And it was from him that she developed her passion for mysticism.

James was famous for several sculptures depicting figures of Greek and Norse mythology. His interest extended beyond Zeus and Thor, however, to include gods and monsters from Indian, Asian, and Eastern European traditions. His depth of knowledge dazzled Florence. Spiritualism was in vogue during the early twentieth century, and she read widely on the subject—books by mediums and skeptics and, importantly, the wellness doctrine of Stanford Kayo. She came to understand her artistic talent as a divine gift, proof that she could be a unique and powerful spiritual vessel. She conducted rituals of purification, preparing her body to be a godly host.

In her free time, she painted an elaborate series of canvases in tribute to Morrigan, the Celtic goddess of death and fate. She explained to James her concept for exhibiting the work—she would nail each piece to a wooden stake in the desert then set fire to them as a sacrifice. As a sculptor who worked in bronze, James's work would practically last forever, and he expressed a perverse delight at the idea of destroying pieces as masterful as Florence's paintings. He communicated her plans to an art promoter he knew in Chicago, and three days later that man stepped into James's shop and into Florence's life. He was Sebastian Greely, the future love of her life.

Greely was small and slender and more beautiful than he was handsome. His family's money allowed him to buy his way into the artistic circles which Florence had struggled for so many years to enter. He was a minor artist himself who bought museums in major U.S. cities and staged arts festivals to show off the work of his more talented friends. Later, he would claim that by merely working in Florence's presence, he'd become several times the artist he would otherwise have been. Having seen the power of her influence in his own work, Greely had no choice but to believe her when she declared herself to be divine.

In the hands of Greely, Florence's desert art fire became the event of the season for those who were fashionable enough to be invited, a group of two dozen artists and poets and art groupies. The show began at dusk and by midnight the last of the paintings had been set ablaze, streaming orange flames upward to honor the heavens. Soon enough, the crowd broke up, leaving Florence and Greely alone in the desert. They made love on the remnants of her work, their bodies becoming smudged by the ash of canvases whose quality rivaled those hanging in any of the world's finest museums.

Florence would go on to inspire every painting of consequence Greely ever made. She was his spiritual guide, converting him to her mystical beliefs. She encouraged him to sell several of his properties and invest in the wellness center that had been abandoned by Stanford Kayo, reimagining it as a retreat for their friends and contemporaries. At first, he refused. Florence responded by leaving him. They were apart for nearly a year.

In the Fall, he wrote to her agreeing to the purchase under the single condition that she return to him. Later, he claimed the statue of Imogene Kayo was what ultimately sold him on the idea. He admired the way she watched over The Castle from her perch, so divine in appearance, like a tribute to Morrigan herself. Florence only nodded when he made this observation. "See, baby?" she said, "the goddess was calling us here. The Castle is where she means for us to be."

VI.

All at once, this memory blinked off.

There was a problem at The Castle. Our body wasn't healed yet, but we had to wake up. We had to wake up. We had to wake up. We had to wake up. We had to wake up. We had to wake up. We had to wake up. We had to wake up. We had to wake up. We had to wake up. We had to wake up. We had to wake up. We had to wake up. We had to wake—

CHAPTER: 08

I.

Our body began to stir. We might have slept for days if we'd had the luxury, but Roma was proving to be a bad influence, coaxing Sam out onto the window ledge because she was too afraid to go meddling through our room without her.

Sam had never known herself to have a fear of heights. Still, watching her step through the window, we felt her certainty that you didn't need a special fear of something to know when risking it was a bad idea. When you're shimmying across a second-story window ledge with no railing, for example. Worse yet, when it's after dark and you have no light to guide you. She didn't need a phobia or the omen of a great blue heron to recognize she'd made a terrible decision.

"What are you doing back there?" Roma called back to her. "What's that sound you're making?"

"No," Sam said, "no." It didn't make sense as an answer to her question, but it was exactly what she meant to communicate. Her back was pressed against The Castle's exterior wall. We felt its flaky bricks scratching against her palms and snagging her clothes as she sidestepped away from her window, toward ours.

Ahead of her, Roma began moving down the center of the ledge like she'd spent a good portion of her life on a tight rope or swinging on a trapeze. "Do you need me to hold your hand?" she asked.

"Don't touch me!" Sam said. "Don't you dare touch me!" She pushed harder against the wall, afraid the words she'd spoken might pull her body toward the edge. She pictured herself curling forward, head first, like a piece of burning paper, floating off into the night. She continued to inch sideways, vaguely aware that she was silently combining swear words and words of prayer.

When she felt confident enough to look up from her feet, she saw Roma crouched in front of our apartment's open living room window. We'd left it cracked that afternoon after Sam's visit. Roma was struggling to raise it further, exerting herself carelessly as if she were standing on solid ground rather than on a piece of one-hundred-and-twenty-year-old masonry which was never meant to hold the weight of two human beings. "We're in!" she said when she finally got it to budge.

"God, shit! God, shit! God, shit!" Sam muttered as she edged toward her. Eventually, she felt the firmness of the windowsill against her lower back, and then a hand was grabbing for her legs through the open window. She kicked back instinctively and nearly struck Roma in the face with her shoe. Then she crouched, taking comfort in the feeling of Roma's arms around her waist, pulling her away from danger. A moment later, they were both on the couch, awkwardly entangled, safe for now.

II.

We had to pull tape off our eyes to open them. We lay in the hospital bed, staring absently until our vision focused, balancing what we were seeing with our eyes with the visions still playing in our head. When we withdrew the IV needle from our arm, a drop ran down our skin, a mix of blood and saline. Soon, we felt strong enough to sit up. The chair beside the bed was empty. We were alone in the room. Our paper hospital gown made a crinkling sound when we adjusted our body and dropped our legs over the side of the bed. A plastic clip on our finger measured our heartbeat on a rolling monitor. The monitor flatlined when we removed it, but no alarm sounded. There seemed to be no alert to anyone on the hospital staff that, according to their machines, our heart was no longer beating. We drank an entire pitcher of water from a rolling table beside the bed. No one came to check on us.

We slid off the bed and rose to our feet, testing our weight on our legs. We were unsteady at first, but we weren't as weak as we'd feared. We found our clothes balled in the room's windowsill and grabbed our shoes, then we locked ourselves inside our small bathroom. For a long time, we stared into the mirror above the sink. The person who stared back at us was ordinary, boring Milo Selby. No sign of Florence could be seen in those eyes because she was deeper inside the body than she'd ever previously been. Not yet permanent, but deep, nonetheless. Our ultimate union would come once we'd completed our work at The Castle, but we had each grown strong enough to hold on to the other. If we were holding on, nothing could separate us.

We relieved our bladder then began to dress. The shoes were the hardest thing. Pulling them on made us lightheaded, but once that feeling had passed, we were fully dressed, on our feet and ready to go home.

We were halfway to the elevators when a voice echoed from behind us, "Milo? You're awake? What the hell are you doing?"

We turned to see Jack coming back to the room, probably from chatting up nurses or emotionally fragile women in the hospital's waiting areas. He had a lidded paper cup of coffee in one hand. "I'm fine," we said. Our voice was hoarse. "I want to go home."

"Home? You can't go home, bro. We need to tell somebody you're awake. They need to check you out before they'll release you."

"That'll take hours," we said. "I'm fine to go now." Jack said nothing, just stared at us like we were a riddle he was trying to solve. "Do you really want to wait here all night for them to release me when we could just leave right now?"

He wiped his hand down his face, considering. He had a day's growth of beard, and the skin around his eyes looked puffy and mottled. "Well, I'll bet half the testing they'd want to do would just be an excuse to pad the bill, the frigging sharks. So, I mean…if you say you're okay, I guess that's cool with me."

"I say I'm okay," we said, then walked to the bank of elevators and hit the down button.

Jack followed behind us. He noticed our clothes and snorted. "What's with the tucked in T-shirt?" he asked. "Do you have a job interview tonight? Or are you on your way to church?"

We said nothing. Despite his bluster, we felt his nervousness.

In the elevator car, he stayed as far from us as he could get, awkwardly fitting himself into a corner. He sensed something about us should alarm him, but he couldn't figure precisely what it was. We were five flights up, and the ride down seemed to take forever. "You know," he said, "you really had me worried. You're all the family I've got, little brother. You can't scare me like that again, you know?"

This was a lie. Jack hadn't been worried. We could see into him just the same as we could see into Sam and Roma and every other resident of The Castle. Jack would have adapted easily if we'd died in our hospital bed—though he might have preferred us to expire on the floor of the common room, twitching and seizing; it would have saved him a drive. We knew he had a recurring fantasy about the car accident that killed Mom and Dad. In the fantasy, he was awoken by a call saying, "Your mom is dead and your dad, and your little brother, Milo." We felt his relief when he imagined those five extra words—*and your little brother, Milo.* To Jack, those words meant freedom.

When we got to the first-floor lobby, he turned to us and asked, "You're sure you're good, right? I don't want to have to explain myself for busting you out of here if you turn around and die on me."

We looked him in the eye, so he knew we were confident. We held his gaze to ease his mind. "No Jack. I'm not going to die."

III.

"God! Get off me! You weigh a thousand pounds," Roma was saying. She had just pulled Sam in through our window, and their bodies were still entwined.

Sam felt the giddy rush of endorphins from having escaped the window ledge without falling to her death. "You're the one with your hands around me," she said, playfully slapping the hand on her waist.

"Grow up," Roma said, letting go and pushing Sam's body away. "Come on, let's find what he's hiding." She did a gymnastic move, flipping onto her feet and causing Sam to tumble face down on the floor. Not wanting to be left alone in our living room, Sam scrambled to her feet. When she caught up to her, Roma was standing in the open doorway of our bedroom. "He's tidy, for a boy."

Following her into our room, Sam was instantly struck by the smell of oil paint. We'd made sure to leave no canvases visible, but that smell alone was confirmation that we'd been lying to her.

Despite having masterminded this break-in, Roma was now unsure about exactly what proof they were looking for. She walked to our desk and started opening drawers as if the odor of paint didn't make it clear what they were after.

Sam scanned the room. Just like in her own bedroom, the closet was shallow. That meant there was only one place where we could have hidden canvases. She walked to our bed and crouched beside it. The smell strengthened. She touched her fingers to the floor under our bed and inched them forward, hoping to avoid placing her hand in drying paint. Her fingertips discovered the blanket. Pulling on it gently, she dragged the edges of several canvases into view.

IV.

"Do you know what the doctors' theory was?" Jack asked. "That it was a growth spurt. Can you believe that? Flipping out the way you did because of a growth spurt?" It was after dark when we left the hospital. On the car ride back to The Castle, Jack was quiet, other than occasional, inane chatter like this.

We answered with the appropriate grunts and clipped answers of a healthy teenager.

When we finally arrived home, we wanted nothing more than to get back to our bedroom and the work we were so close to finishing, but Brandon, Fish and Dr. Rimini rushed to us as soon as we stepped into the building.

V.

Upstairs, Sam called to Roma, "Here! I found it."

Roma moved to the bed and quickly took stock of what she had uncovered. "Pull from the other end," Sam said, directing Roma to the head of the bed.

Together, they pulled the blanket across the floor, bringing to light dozens of painted canvases, arranged in stacks.

"Oh my God," Roma said, "he's amazing."

"Florence has been painting through him. That's how she's communing with him. I think that's how she's gotten so strong."

Sam was staring down at the stacks, trying to make sense of them when Roma asked, "That's my ear, isn't it?"

Sam looked where she was pointing and saw a small canvas with an up close, intricate rendering of a human ear. Three studs in the lobe and a silver orbital ring, just like Roma's. "It looks like it."

"But I mean…why is he painting me?"

"He's painting all of us." Sam pointed to a separate canvas. It was the lower third of a small face which clearly belonged to one of the twins. Something about the arrangement of the open mouth made her skin crawl.

Roma stared at the two portraits, failing to make sense of them. Finally, she said, "We need to lay these out."

The top canvases were still wet. When they pulled them from the stacks, the paintings beneath were tacky, dry enough not to smear easily, but not yet fully set. "He must have been making more than one of these every day since he moved in," Sam said. "Way more than one per day." With Florence's guiding hand, she knew this was possible. Still, she was surprised by our obvious commitment to this work.

The paintings were a tapestry, large and small canvases that fit together like a puzzle to form a larger image. They began by laying them out on the floor, but soon had to spread them out with some pieces laid across the bed and others jutted up against the far wall. They rearranged them, moving certain canvases here or there before settling on their appropriate placement. As they worked, they were amazed to see how purple shadows became the cut of a cheekbone and bands of pink and black formed photorealistic mouths when viewed in the context of neighboring canvases. Slowly, faces began to take shape, faces they knew—Jack, Fish, the twins, Roma, Dr. Rimini. Some of the pieces were small, painted on scraps of cardboard from old notebooks or on the white interiors of microwavable food boxes. Given their size, those pieces tended to be the least clear and required concentration to find where they belonged. Sam was deeply invested in finding a home for the small beige and red rectangle she was holding when she realized Roma had stopped working. She looked up at her and asked, "Are you just going to stand there and watch me do this? There are so many more of these to figure out."

Roma didn't respond, just continued to stare down at the canvases.

Concerned, Sam rose to take in the larger image they were building. She quickly understood what about it had caused Roma's reaction. The scene was claustrophobic—the residents crammed together unnaturally, toppling into each other like cartoonish drunks from old black and white movies. It was obvious they'd been posed this way in the corner of a room with a dirt floor. It was obvious all of them were dead. Several gaps remained. They had yet to find Dr. Rimini's left cheek, for example, and Fish's right hand, and Sam was missing entirely. With a trembling hand, she reached forward and placed the tan card where she now saw it belonged. When she rose again, those splotches of pigment had become a gory slash in Roma's throat.

"Sam…" Roma said from beside her. Before she could say more, they heard sounds coming from outside our apartment. She grabbed Sam's arm and squeezed. The sounds quickly registered as keys in the door followed by movement inside the apartment. They heard Jack's voice.

"Shit!" Roma whispered. "Shit!"

With no hesitation, Sam began pulling her toward the bedroom window, which she forced open with pure adrenaline. Roma went first, then Sam clambered out behind her onto the ledge. She had just pulled the window most of the way down when she saw a flash of us enter our room to appraise the scene they'd left behind.

VI.

"Oh my God, you're back," Fish had said. "We assumed they would at least keep him overnight. How is he? He looks good."

Jack, who was never one for small talk, handled each question with as short an answer as possible. He told them we were tired and needed to get straight to bed. Soon enough, they took the hint.

We allow Jack to go ahead of us on the stairs. Sam and Roma were in our room learning the nature of our work, but that didn't mean we were in a rush to catch them. They already knew. The damage was done. The best thing was to proceed sensibly.

As we climbed the stairs, Florence showed me a flicker of memory from long ago when Salvador Dalí smuggled a pregnant donkey into the building then stood back, horrified, as it gave birth to a mewling foal on The Castle's second-floor landing.

"I thought they'd never leave us alone," Jack said when we were standing at our apartment door.

Once inside, we said in as natural a tone as we could manage, "I'll be in my room." When we got to our bedroom door, we hesitated for a moment, quietly knocking twice with one knuckle to give Sam and Roma time to escape before we pushed the door open.

We were standing inside our bedroom, appraising the harm they had done when Jack appeared in the doorway behind us. "Hey, man, do you—" he started. He was close enough to see what we were looking at, all our work laid out across the floor and the bed, and it made him go momentarily silent. When he finally spoke, his voice had grown loud and thorny: "What in the hell is this? Is that—Jesus, Milo, is that *me?*" He shoved us, hard. "Are you sick in the head or something? Why would you paint this? What the hell is wrong with you?"

We understood then. It was Jack. It had come earlier than we'd expected, before our work was technically completed, but it was time to consummate our union. Jack had volunteered to be our first.

We turned to face him. We smiled and said, "I've been painting again, big brother." We swept our arm around the room to invite him to look at all we'd done. "Aren't they the cat's meow?"

"I want you to explain this right now, Milo." We felt his growing fear. "Right now, do you hear me?"

"They weren't meant to be seen," we said, "not until they were done. But *c'est la vie.*" We moved toward him like a predatory animal, forcing him to press his body against the wall. We were face to face, an inch apart.

"This is nuts," he said. "You're sick, bro. You're crazy." He turned his head to gain a fraction of distance from us.

He was such a boring cliché. The sibling abuser. The bully who wears his bluster like a mask to hide how frightened and pathetic he feels inside. We couldn't help but laugh at him. "Crazy? Oh…I don't know, maybe." A globule of our spit stood in a pyramid of bubbles on his chin.

He responded poorly to the feeling of our hands on him. He'd come to understand the gravity of his situation, and he screamed and screamed. But we were claws and teeth. We were an ancient natural force. We were more than capable of subduing and conquering. We could end the life of a pathetic mouse like Jack with the snap of our fingers. And, just like snapping our fingers, we did.

VII.

When we were through, we pressed our body against the wall between our bed and the window, back-to-back with Sam and Roma where they hid on the ledge. Jack's screaming had been so pained and unexpected it sent a jolt through Sam's body, and Roma had needed to reach out to brace her for fear she would fall. We were relieved she hadn't.

To get back to Sam's bedroom, they would need to pass in front of our open living room window. Neither had dared risk it, afraid we would see them, unaware we were already watching them now.

"He killed him," Sam said in a panicky whisper. "What do we do? What do we do?" She crouched, rocking her body forward and back, the way she used to as a toddler when her emotions grew too big.

"I know. I know, but you need to calm down." Roma said. Her voice tremored. We felt just how far from calm she was herself.

In the silence that followed Jack's screaming, Sam devolved into full, nose-running sobs, heaving so forcefully she began to feel lightheaded, a perilous state to be in for someone balancing so high off the ground.

Roma took her wrist to stop her from beating her palm against her temple. "We can't do anything for him now. We need to focus on saving ourselves and the others."

Sam hadn't been thinking of the others, but the realization came to her now like a slap in the face. "Dad!" she said, loud enough that Roma shushed her. "If he came back up to the apartment, he would have heard the screaming. What if he comes to check it out?"

Roma looked like she was going to rebuke her, to tell her she was hysterical and needed to calm down. She didn't though. She knew she was right. They stared together at Sam's open bedroom window. It was twenty feet from them, but it felt so far away. "We're going to have to move fast. If he sees us—"

"I know." She was already inching up the wall, getting to her feet. "I'll go fast. Come on. Let's go. I'm ready."

Roma stepped toward our living room window and crouched slightly to peek into it. "I don't see him," she whispered. This made us smile.

Sam nodded. "Fast," she confirmed.

Roma mouthed the word then abruptly turned and jogged past our window. A second later, she disappeared into Sam's bedroom. Sam followed her, fear for her father outweighing her fear of falling. She sprinted to her window, and Roma backed into the room to make space for her. Sam ducked into the opening, but in her haste, she banged her head hard against the window frame. The pain caused her legs to buckle, and her knees sang out in pain as they smacked against the concrete. She felt Roma's hands on her, pulling her onto her bedroom floor. She landed with a thump on the paint-covered rug.

She woke up on the floor understanding she'd lost time. Twenty or thirty seconds according to Roma. She blinked her eyes into focus then dragged herself to her feet and ran clumsily past Roma, all through the apartment, calling out to Dr. Rimini.

No answer came.

She was already at her front door when Roma called, "Sam, wait! You can't go over there!"

Ignoring her, Sam pulled the door open and hurried into the hall. Roma didn't try to stop her when she arrived at our apartment door. She only hung back, watching her like Sam had wandered into a mine field she was unwilling to enter herself. We had come into our living room, thrillingly close to her. We watched as our doorknob turned, and we smiled when she found it locked. She was considering knocking when Dr. Rimini's voice called to her from down the hall.

He was at the top of the stairs. She hurried toward him, meeting him in the middle of the hallway. "Dad," she cried, falling into his arms.

"Sam?" We felt his confusion and worry. He hugged her for only a moment before grasping her shoulders and holding her at an arm's distance. "What happened, honey? You're bleeding."

She hadn't realized she was bleeding until that moment, but now she saw the new scrapes on her knees. He hadn't been talking about her knees, though. He extended a finger and placed it lightly in her hair. The sting of his touch made her shudder. When he pulled it away, his fingertip was coated in a shiny slick of blood.

"Was this him?" he asked, referring to the ghost of Stanford Kayo. "Did he do this to you? I'm so sorry, honey. I shouldn't have let you go into the apartment without me. I thought you were going to Roma's." He clutched her to him, and we experienced the complicated feeling of that moment—pain from her injured body mixed with the comfort of his touch, the fear for his daughter's safety mingled with the shame of having failed her. Sam had a flash memory of how she used to run to her mom with a cut or scrape or when she woke up in the night with a sour stomach. Her absence was in their embrace too.

After a moment, Sam said, "Nothing happened, Dad. Nothing supernatural, I mean."

"Then how did you get so beaten up?" Here, he turned his attention to Roma who was still standing in their doorway. "Were you girls fighting?"

"She fell," Roma said in a voice which approximated her usual coolness. "We weren't fighting, just horsing around. It was my fault. It's nothing serious, though. Right, Sam?"

"I'm fine," Sam said. She offered Dr. Rimini a smile to help him along in believing her.

"We were about to check with Milo to see if he has any band aids," Roma continued. "They just got back."

Dr. Rimini's forehead creased. "Sam, don't you still have bandages from the hospital?"

"Oh, no, I…ran out," she lied. "They didn't give me that many."

Roma came to them and gently took Sam by the wrist, coaxing her away from him. "You know, now that I think about it, I remember packing some bandages and antibacterial stuff when I left home. Do you want to come with me, Sam, and I'll get you cleaned up?"

The offer hung in the air. A different sort of parent might have forbidden Sam from going, insisting on tending to her himself. But Dr. Rimini and Sam both knew he wasn't that parent. Tragedy had changed them from a family to a partnership, a unit of two, and he'd come to think of himself as Sam's equal as much as her protector. This left the decision to her. We stood, awaiting her answer. She was torn. We felt how strongly she wished she could tell her father everything—the danger we posed, the suffering we would cause them all—with the confidence that she could then just relax and leave this horror for him to solve. As much as she wished for it, though, she didn't possess that confidence.

"Dad, I'm going to go with Roma, okay? It's just some scrapes and a bump on the head. Why don't you go to bed? I have my key, so you can lock the door. I might hang out with her for a while. So just…just be sure to lock the door, okay?"

VIII.

We sat on the edge of the tub, looking at our hands. They were sticky with blood. Our mouth tasted coppery, and the tight feeling of the skin on our face suggested blood was drying there too.

For the first time since she'd taken over my body, Florence loosened her grip on me just enough to make a sliver of separation between my will and hers. She became like a tiny voice whispering in my ear. *Rebecca Steiner,* that voice whispered. *Jack hated you because of Rebecca, Milo. Probably, he's always hated you, ever since you were born. Her death was just a convenience for him, a way to justify what he always felt about you… He called you crazy. Jack hated you so much he would have sent you away someday. He'd have sent you away, forever…* Florence had died in one of those places you go when you're sent away forever, and the scenes she showed me from her experiences there were terrifying. We'd only done what was needed, she reminded me. We'd done what was necessary. I nodded, unsure, and she tightened her hold again, bringing us back together.

There was much to do, but first we needed to shower. We stood and stripped then turned on the faucet. We stepped into the bathtub and closed our eyes to the pinkness of the draining water.

Once we were rinsed clean, we returned to our bedroom, naked and dripping. We avoided the mass on the floor, keeping our back to it as we stood at the dresser and pulled on a T-shirt and jeans.

The clothes stuck to our wet body as we moved down the hallway, but the night air from the open living room window had left the apartment uncomfortably warm, and the cling of them began to release by the time we got to Jack's bedroom.

We sat on his bed. Our first sacrifice had left us fatigued, and we needed to rest. A part of us desperately wished we hadn't begun this work. It begged for us to stop before we hurt anyone else. The stronger part strangled those thoughts, pushing them deep into us where the nuisance of them wouldn't be heard.

We closed our eyes and settled in for a nap. Once everyone was asleep, we could finish what we'd started. For now, Florence allowed me to see the last time she'd attempted this work.

The year was 1947. She and Greely had been running the artist's retreat for nearly a year. This was a fruitful time in Greely's creative life. Aided by Florence, he was producing the best work of his career. She was happy to give him the credit. Her personal ambitions were now entirely in her spiritual work, devoting herself to becoming a perfect vessel for the goddess.

She researched the indigenous people of the land The Castle was built on. After several failed attempts, she successfully put herself into a trance with the aid of herbs which were used in those peoples' religious ceremonies. While in this trance, the goddess spoke to her in a voice which was clear and unmistakable. Florence communed with her for two full days before waking up—drowning in sweat and covered in her own filth—with the goddess's words still ringing in her mind: "Immortalize the lambs and baptize yourself in blood and fire." For weeks, Florence pondered this, wondering how she might spill a quantity of blood large enough to satisfy the goddess's great hunger. The answer proved to be right under her nose.

The Castle's artists routinely came and went, but seven resided there currently. Florence focused her planning on only those seven. Ignoring Greely's protests, she stepped away from his work and locked herself in an empty studio where she began to paint. She made portrait after portrait of the residents, Greely included, caught in scenes of agony and horror.

During this time, she barely ate or spoke to anyone. When she wasn't painting, she took long walks across the grounds, attuning herself to the land's natural energies, searching for the most hospitable location for the ceremony she needed to perform. In the woods beyond the pond, she found a vibration that intrigued her. She closed her eyes, listening to the pitch and rhythm of that place, allowing it to call her to where it was strongest.

It led her deep into the woods where she discovered a stone building with a heavy metal door. The spiritual power of that structure was overwhelming. It nearly took her breath. She knew, having read Stanford Kayo's books on spiritual wellness, that she had found his deprivation sauna. In his words, he'd built it to be 'an underground chamber, dark as a womb and free of all external distractions, where patients enter for hours or days and from which they emerge reborn, having shed their most unhealthful impulses.' He claimed his guests entered willingly, but the energy of the place suggested to Florence that very bad things had happened there. She felt screaming people locked inside for days at a time against their will. It would be perfect for her needs.

CHAPTER:09

I.

Roma really did have bandages and ointment. Sam followed her to her apartment and straight into her bathroom where Roma nodded for her to take a seat on the closed toilet lid. Sam sat and waited as she rifled through the medicine cabinet. She glanced at the cabinet's open mirrored door before quickly looking away, afraid it would fog like the mirror in her own bathroom and show her something new and sinister she didn't care to see. From the cabinet, Roma produced a metal box of band aids and a blood red bottle of antiseptic with a spray top which looked like it might have been as old as The Castle itself. She placed the items on the edge of the sink then grabbed a washcloth from her towel bar. She made a ritual of wetting the cloth under the warming tap and wringing it out in the basin. Sam came to realize she was stalling, repeating this action again and again to avoid having to look her in the eye. It made sense to her; Sam didn't want to confront this nightmare either.

Eventually, Roma turned off the tap and crouched in front of her. She draped the washcloth over her index finger and pressed it lightly against the scrapes on Sam's knees, one by one. We felt the sting of the cloth on Sam's wounds, the snag of its fibers against her broken skin. Roma kept silent and focused as she worked. When she was through, she rose and tossed the washcloth into the sink basin and turned the tap on again, leaving the water on to run over it. From her metal box, she chose two square adhesive bandages. She unwrapped them and laid them in Sam's lap before grabbing and shaking her ancient red bottle. She crouched and locked eyes with Sam. "This is going to hurt like hell."

"Okay." Sam raised her face to the ceiling and squeezed her eyes shut. She heard the whooshing sound of liquid spraying out of the bottle, then her eyes shot open again, cartoonishly wide. "Ah-ha-ha-ha!" she said, an expression of pain that sounded like a try at some movie villain's sinister cackle. The liquid was bubbling red on her knees. "What is that stuff?" she demanded.

In place of an answer, Roma brought her face an inch from Sam's lesions and blew. The gesture was so unexpected and motherly it nearly worked to distract Sam from the feeling that her skin had been set on fire. "Better?"

"Sure…I think so."

Roma lifted the band-aids from her lap and set about removing the wax paper from their adhesive backing and applying one to each of her knees. "It's mercurochrome," she said belatedly. "I stole it from my grandma's bathroom cabinet when she died. It feels like acid on an open wound, but there's nothing better." She rose and placed the bottle back inside the medicine cabinet, then she turned off the faucet and rung out the washcloth. "Okay, let's see that scalp." She took Sam's chin in her hand, using it to steer her head in one direction then the other as she appraised the gash in her hair. "You've got about an inch-long split. Look down at your lap."

Sam did as she was told, spreading her knees so Roma didn't bump them with her own while she worked. She felt Roma's fingers delicately part her hair. Only then, when her head was down and they were in no danger of their eyes meeting, did Roma begin to discuss the situation facing them. "So," she said, "Florence Massey is going to kill us all."

Reflexively, Sam's head jerked up, but Roma pushed it down again with her fingertips. "We need to warn everyone." she said. Her chin was tucked tightly against her throat, lending a strange pitch to her voice. Her words sounded slurred. "You could go bang on Fish and Brandon's door, and I could get Dad, and we can tell them we have to get out."

"Do you think they'd believe us? Your dad would, probably. Or at least he'd humor you. Fish and Brandon wouldn't. Honestly, though, if they chose to stick around here and get eaten by the monster or whatever, I'd say that was on them. If it weren't for—"

"The twins," Sam said, finishing the thought. "We wouldn't have to say it's supernatural, though, right? We could tell them there's a fire. We could *start* a fire. Then they wouldn't have a choice."

Roma snickered.

"What?"

"I just can't believe I'm the one voting against burning my problems to the ground. Fun as it would be, I doubt it would solve anything. Milo could evacuate the building just as easily as the rest of us. And if he can carry Florence out with him, what then? She kills us on the lawn while we watch The Castle burn?"

She was right. Sam knew she was.

"Speaking of Fish and Brandon, though," Roma said, pressing the washcloth to Sam's scalp, "I found something out about them tonight."

"Seriously? When? What did you find out?"

"Did you honestly believe I went to the kitchen for a midnight snack? I mean, Brandon's a decent chef, but he leans a little heavily on braised dead flesh for my taste."

"Fair. So, what were you really doing?"

"I was breaking into Fish's office." She said it matter-of-factly, like it was no big deal.

"What?" Roma didn't resist this time when Sam's head shot up. A loose end of the washcloth draped over her eyes and nose. She swiped it to one side to reveal Roma looking back at her, a smug grin on her face. "You broke into his office?" She whispered these words as if someone might hear her, unaware someone already could.

"Mm-hmm. It's tucked back there behind the kitchen. I think it used to be a curing room or something. And I'd stolen the key from him earlier, so maybe *breaking in* makes it sound a little more badass than the moment deserves. It was more like…taking a tour. I was *helping myself to a tour* of Fish's office when I overheard your dad yelling at them."

"He wasn't yelling, really," Sam said. "But, whatever—what did you find?"

"Put your head down," Roma said, pleased with the reaction she'd gotten and drawing it out. "I'll bet they'd give you a couple of stitches if you went to the hospital. You're going to have a gnarly scar, but if you ever shave your head, it'll look bitchin. Seriously, though, put your head down. I need to stop the bleeding."

Sam bowed her head. "Tell me what you found," she slurred.

"A lot of clutter, mostly. I looked through his desk and in his filing cabinets. All I found were real estate documents and contractor invoices for all the remodeling they've done to the place. But on his laptop—"

"Fish has a laptop?"

"Keep your head down," Roma scolded. "I didn't mean for that to be some big reveal. It wouldn't connect to the Internet. They're not hoarding WI-FI or anything. And before you ask, no, I'm not some master hacker. He's a technophobe. His password is all-caps 'PASSWORD' for God's sake." She raised the washcloth from Sam's scalp, examining the wound, then said, "The blood is slowing. That's good." She returned to the sink, tossing the soiled cloth into the basin.

Sam worked out a crick in her neck while Roma searched again through the medicine cabinet. "Okay, so, for the last time, what did you find?"

"Well, do you know that story he tells about when they first advertised the community, how he was nervous they'd get a million applicants, but barely anyone applied?"

"Yeah," Sam said. "He told us that when we took our tour."

"Of course, he did. It's one of his chestnuts."

Roma was right. He'd told us this story too.

Sam continued, "I remember he said he had a dream where he was 'literally drowning' in applications."

Roma came back to her with a tube of antibacterial gel. "The thing is, he has a folder of applications saved to his desktop." She squeezed a knob of gel onto her finger. Sam lowered her head, this time without being told. "When I opened it, I saw thousands of responses. And I mean *thousands*. Not just from America, either. Applicants from Canada, Mexico. I even saw a few from Europe. Maybe other places too. I stopped looking." She'd slathered Sam's cut with gel and now stepped back, rubbing the remainder into her hands like lotion.

Sam met her eyes. "Why would he claim there were no replies? He says the thing about everyone being too slavish to technology to be interested."

Roma smiled devilishly. "A bald-faced lie, as it turns out."

"Maybe all those applications were new."

"I thought of that too, but the most recent files were saved weeks ago. I went to his browsing history, and he hasn't even connected to the Internet in almost a month."

Sam stared at the floor, trying and failing to understand. "I'm confused. What does this mean?"

Roma sat on the rim of the tub. "Well, I obviously don't know for sure, but it seems clear the two families they did pick were chosen for a reason."

"I don't understand. Dad and I are just regular people. What's the reason?"

Roma arched her eyebrows, encouraging her to think harder. "Would you say you have anything in common with someone here? Possibly with a certain possessed little shithead?"

"You mean painting?"

Roma tempered her nod with a shrug which suggested it was only a guess.

"But that doesn't make sense, does it? I mean, in thousands of applicants, surely hundreds of people listed their hobby as art. There must be a million old hippies who do folk art and would love to be a part of a place like this. It can't have just been me and Milo."

"True. But art isn't the only thing you two have in common, is it? Do you know about his mom and dad? And that girl who died? I can show you their application. It was—"

"Tragic. Yeah, I know."

"I can't claim that this is a fully formed theory, but if Florence Massey feeds off creativity and tragedy, then you and Milo must be like a banquet for her."

Sam nodded to herself. She sounded numb when she said, "So, you're saying she used me until someone even sadder and more messed up came along? Which means…if Milo *hadn't* come along…"

"I'd probably be sitting here by myself trying to figure out how to stop you from killing everyone."

Sam absently chewed her lip. "What about you, then?" she asked. "If we were chosen for a reason, how do you fit in?"

"Me?" Roma laughed. "I'm not part of anyone's plan. I just happened to crash the party. I'm just Florence's bad luck."

Sam nodded. "And Fish and Brandon?"

"Those two," she said as a slow sigh. "I actually have no idea about those two. I mean, I see how it looks like a conspiracy. They could be masterminding it, I guess, but I just can't see them playing any kind of role here. Fish is such a doofus, and Brandon's sweet but clueless. My guess is they tried to open this place with the best of intentions, and Florence just manipulated the process. We know she can do things like that, if she's somehow really a lamia. Fish and Brandon probably didn't even know. I can't quite picture a situation where Fish sees a ghost and manages to keep his mouth shut about it. He'd have called one of those ghost hunting shows within an hour just to get on TV."

We felt Sam's weariness, how her thoughts had become clouded. She experienced a passing resentment toward Roma. The thought was irrational, she knew, but if Roma hadn't come to The Castle and crashed the party, Sam wouldn't need to know any of this. She could just walk down the hall and get her dad and somehow convince him to leave with her and never look back. It would be hard to live with herself if she walked away and let everyone die. But at least she'd be alive to feel that guilt. "So, what do we do now?" She blinked away tears.

Roma swallowed hard, but her eyes were cold and steely. "Now," she said, "we kill Milo."

Sam was the only one of us who hadn't known this was her plan.

II.

We were lying on Jack's bed, watching this exchange. The room was dark. Visions of them had stirred us from our sleep. From time to time, our eyelids would flutter in short bursts of rest before we would startle awake again and return our attention to the plot being formed against us.

In our brief dreams, images from Florence's life came in fragments—her father, drunk and violent; flying hands and elbows and wild shouts; her father's two hands morphing into the hands of many. His thick, accented voice became the chorus of an angry crowd, all of them directing their rage at Florence. We looked up at them through her eyes. She was crouched protectively on ground which was soft and wet. Blood, not hers, covered her hands. Sebastian Greely's blood. This was how her previous attempt at the ritual had ended. She'd completed one sacrificial killing—the same progress we'd made so far with Jack— before she'd been overpowered by the other artists. As the memory of this horrific scene played out, her grip on me loosened. It was like the emotions tied to this memory caused her to forget herself. In that margin of space, I formed a thought which was only mine. *She's recalling this because she's afraid she'll fail again tonight.*

The thought was mine, but Florence heard me think it. All at once, she clamped me tight again, squeezing, momentarily stealing breath from the lungs we shared. The images snapped off. Our eyes opened in Jack's dark room. Despite our exhaustion, it was time.

We rose from the bed and moved into the hall. Our bedroom door was open, and we stood in the doorway, staring down at what lay on our floor. It was broken and still, just as we'd left it. We needed to move forward, prepare for the ceremony, but a part of us was hesitant. Our thoughts were in conflict about just what it was we were seeing. Jack? Our parents' only other son, pitiful and tragic despite his dislike for us? No. Merely a lamb. A sacrifice for the goddess so she might live in us and fill the vessel of our body with her greatness. We moved our eyes toward the bedroom window. It was the only way. A part of us found this realization to be chilling. But it would be too dangerous to carry him through the second-floor hallway and down the stairs. He felt nothing now anyway; it wouldn't be cruel. Besides, we hadn't rested for long, and we needed to conserve our energy.

The window was still cracked open from when Sam and Roma had fled in such a hurry. After bringing it up the rest of the way, we stood over the sacrifice with our legs spread wide. We lifted, strong even for two. Still, it was awkward with only two arms slung under its shoulders, its legs dragging between our own, which bowed wide to encircle them. Its head was facing forward, and it bobbed as we dragged it like it was nodding toward the window. Our foot snagged one leg of the cheap easel as we moved, toppling it with a thin metallic clatter. Once at the window, we angled the sacrifice through the opening, lifting and drawing it out onto the ledge. We paused for breath then crouched and stepped out ourselves, careful not to trample on what we'd lain there. The outside air was still and hot.

Kick it, we thought but hesitated to act. More insistent this time: *Kick it off the ledge.* We lifted our foot. A few firm pushes with the bottom of our shoe caused the mass to slide forward until one of its arms was dangling over the edge. A final, hard kick and it slid over, disappearing into the darkness with an eventual muted thump.

We took a deep breath and stared past the bronze statue of Imogene Kayo, toward the pond. Insects chirped in distant trees. Things were going well. We allowed ourselves to smile.

III.

The kitchen clock showed two-seventeen in the morning. Everyone was asleep except for Sam and Roma who were together, still debating the best way to stop us. The kitchen was dark, and a glint of moonlight from the window reflected a million speckles of light across the wall of appliances. We moved through the kitchen to the narrow aisleway which was hidden behind it and stopped at Fish's office door. We tried the door handle and weren't surprised to find it locked. Roma, we knew, had stolen the key, so we returned to the kitchen and grabbed a towel we found draped over the handle of the broad, industrial oven. We doubled it over our right hand and held it tight with our left. Back at the office door, we made a fist, reared back, and smashed the towel into its tall, skinny window. The glass fractured into a spider web of cracks, but it held. We struck it a second time, punching out a circle just big enough to swallow our fist. The hole was jagged all around its rim like we'd stuck our arm down the throat of some monstrous lamprey whose circle of teeth threatened to pierce our wrist. We pulled our arm carefully out of the hole, jostling loose shards which fell and tinkled around our feet where they shattered into tiny diamonds.

Cuts flecked our arm. The towel on our hand bloomed with red spots. We removed it to reveal knuckles that were scraped open from the impact with the window. We clamped the towel around the edges of the hole and snapped off chunks of the fractured glass, letting them drop onto the office floor. When it was large enough, we reached through and unlatched the door.

It swung open into a small, dark room. We had a dim memory of seeing this space long ago when it smelled like smoldering cedar, when a rack of cow ribs and halved pig carcasses hung from its ceiling to cure. We stepped into the cluttered room and straight to the ring of keys we'd come for. Fish kept them on a metal hook above his office desk. Blood from our knuckles dripped onto the paper desk calendar when we reached for them. A part of us reflected on how we'd have once run to our mother with a wound like this. How horrified she would be at the sight of her son's blood. How she would have clutched us to her body and fussed over us. We would have acted like she was being ridiculous while secretly cherishing every second of her attention. Abruptly, our chest constricted like our heart was being squeezed. The feeling caused us to gasp for breath, and that fanciful thought was gone. After our breathing had steadied and our heart had slowed, our only thoughts concerned the task which lay ahead of us and the two girls who were trying uselessly to stop us.

IV.

We opened The Castle's large double doors and stepped out onto the porch. The pavement was covered in the blood of our mother's only other son.

No, merely that of a slaughtered lamb.

As strong as we were, it was tiring dragging the mass from the driveway through the yard, our arms hooked under its armpits. The toes of its sneakers left stuttering ruts in the ground as we disappeared with it into the woods. Under the canopy of trees, the darkness seemed endless. In the distance, we heard animals scurrying in their mindless hunt for food or a mate, still unaware that tonight was a holy night.

We moved into the clearing surrounding the pond, and the sudden glow of the moon felt like a gift from divinity. We trudged on, under that pale light, ignoring the stinging in our muscles from the weight of our load, all the while listening in on Sam and Roma, two more of our lambs.

In the woods on the pond's far side, darkness returned with the upward reach of the trees. We dragged our sacrifice through the tangle of groundcover and over the impediment of a fallen tree trunk which blocked our path. The air surrounding the depravation sauna seemed charged with a field of energy that tickled our skin as we approached it. After laying down our load a few feet from the metal door, we shifted through the keys on Fish's stolen keyring until we found the one we needed. A shaft of moonlight drew our eyes to the name *Milo Selby* written in blood which had faded and browned, and then to *Sam Rimini,* carved into the face of the door, gleaming. A part of us asked, "Why only Sam's name?"

There was an answer, of course, but the stronger part of us withheld it. It wasn't listening or else simply didn't want the curious part of us to know.

V.

While we conducted our business in the woods, Sam was arguing with Roma that they should call the police, that they obviously couldn't commit murder.

Roma believed Sam didn't understand the scope of what they were facing. "What are you going to say when you call?" she asked. "That your friend is possessed by the spirit of a dead woman who's trying to kill us all?"

Sam bristled at the mocking curl of her lip. "I'll just say I want to report a murder."

"And then what? They come and arrest him, and he spends the rest of his life in prison with Florence rotting away inside him like a cancer?"

Sam winced at the indelicate reference to the disease that had so recently taken her mother. Roma realized how tactless the question had been, but she held her eyes on Sam, anyway. No time for hurt feelings now.

She'd gotten her point across though. For months, Sam watched her mother wither away as her cancer rampaged through her. The first changes were physical—a loss of weight and color. After she'd become bedridden, Sam would ignore her constant readjustments as she tried for a comfortable position inside a body that would never be comfortable again. Over time, she lost her speech—at first, for hours or days at a time, before becoming permanently mute. Her hair was gone from the endless rounds of unsuccessful treatments. The worst were the changes to her face. A dulling and bruising of her eyes. Her mouth perpetually open, and her jaw cocked sharply to one side. Staring into her mother's face in those final days, Sam couldn't find the woman who'd raised and protected her, taught her to love birds and painting, her life's most important person. She only saw a monster from a scary movie. It became a challenge not to pray for death to put an end to her suffering. Sam couldn't live with herself if her inaction condemned us to a similar fate. "Okay," she relented, "not the police then. But there's got to be something else. Why couldn't we just do an exorcism?"

"Are you a priest? Do you know how to do an exorcism?"

"No. But, I mean, we could *call* a priest, right? There are Catholic churches everywhere."

"And, what? Hope you can convince him? Have him come out for a spooky tour of our haunted house, then wait for him to get approval from the Vatican before he can do anything to help? Florence is on a killing spree, Sam. You saw those paintings. You know what she's planning. Anyway, why do people always look to Catholicism to handle possessions? What if the demon or whatever isn't Catholic? It's just silly superstition."

Sam had no answer to this. She felt small under Roma's stern gaze. She hardly meant it when she said, "Maybe we should ask Stanford Kayo what to do…"

For a long time, Roma continued to stare at her, her face unreadable. Eventually, she nodded and turned away, saying, "Worth a shot. I'll grab a mirror."

VI.

They set up the devil's mirror in Roma's bedroom. Even with the stakes of what was facing them, Sam was hesitant to pour a circle of salt onto Roma's floor, like she was doing something naughty that would get her in trouble. Absurdly, she first had to give herself permission by silently resolving to sweep it up once this was all over. After pouring the salt circle, she stepped over its rim and joined Roma's side. Roma lit the last of the candles. The mirror was propped with a stack of textbooks. Her eyes met Sam's in the mirror glass. "Okay, go."

Wasting no time, Sam called, "Um, Stanford Kayo?"

They waited, but no change came to their reflections. They both looked strung out to her, sallow and pale with dark circles forming under their eyes.

Sam struggled to recall the phrasing she'd used during the first summoning. "We command the spirit of Stanford Kayo to show itself in this mirror!" she tried. "We demand his spirit show itself now!"

For several seconds, the only movement in the mirror was from Roma's tired eyes blinking at her. Slowly, though, the glass began to cloud, and Stanford Kayo appeared to them. When he came into focus, his expression looked pained. "It is beginning again," he said with desperation in his high, tinny voice. "It has already begun."

"How can we stop her?" Sam asked, hoping for any option short of murder.

Kayo startled like she'd caught him talking to himself, like he'd only just become aware of her watching him. He pointed his dead eyes at her. "Stop her?"

"Florence. How do we exorcise Florence Massey?"

"No," was all he said. He stared into some distant space which was unavailable to them.

"No?" Roma said. "What do you mean, 'no?' No, what?"

"A mere innocent girl," he said. "A mere lamb. Much like you, I didn't understand. The window to escape has passed, however. Each of you is doomed. Each of you will die tonight."

"That's not true. Tell us how to stop her," Sam demanded.

"Entwined spirits fuse irrevocably. I did not know it," Kayo repeated. "I did not know, Imogene. Forgive me, dear."

"Imogene? What does Imogene have to do with Florence?"

"I communed with the lamia," Kayo wailed. His sorrow recalled Sunday school lessons from Sam's youth—sinners rending their garments. "I brought her to us. But you were so sick, Imogene. I merely wanted to give you strength. I simply wanted you to live. But it took you, Love. And it has stayed here. Disguised as this, disguised as that. A goddess. An artist. Trickster, trickster."

Sam glanced at Roma who was gazing intently into the mirror, a reflection of Sam's own confusion. Unwilling to give up, she stated loudly to the spirit, "We want to know how to exorcise the thing that's taken Milo Selby."

He didn't respond to Sam directly, only reflected in a sighing voice, again as if to himself, "The Spaniard, Dalí believed he needed an exorcism, but the lamia never wanted him. Never him."

"What does this matter?" Sam demanded. She was angry. Her rage made our heart pound behind her eyes. "Tell us how we can stop her!"

Kayo's face was contorted like he was crying, but his dead eyes remained dry. "A spirit cannot be separated from a willing vessel," he said. "I convinced Imogene to be willing. I told her it would heal her, but she was too delicate to contain it. Your friend is not so delicate, and a willing vessel must be shattered. It must be broken by force. The vessel must be destroyed. Get good with God, children. You have mere hours, perhaps only moments. Hug your loved ones. Death is near you all."

Sam's mind was racing. Surely, she could find a way to end this without "shattering" us. This is what she was thinking when the mirror tumbled sideways off the stack of books and landed face down on the carpet. She jumped at the sudden movement, then spun around to face Roma. The position of her body—raised up on the palms of her hands with one leg stretched in front of her—made Sam aware that the mirror hadn't been moved by supernatural forces, but from a natural kick from Roma's black leather boot.

"Asshole," Roma said of Kayo, then she rose and stepped out of the conjuring circle and disappeared down the hall.

When Sam joined her in the living room, she was sitting on her futon, frantically paging through a spiral notebook. "I took notes on this," she said absently.

"Notes on…?"

"Right here!" She read to herself before saying, "Yes. Salvador Dalí had himself exorcised in 1947."

"Is that important right now?"

"Kayo said Dalí had an exorcism. That's true. A month after Greely disappeared, and they shut this place down, Dalí had himself exorcised." She ran her finger over lines of script that were too small for Sam to make out. "He was exorcised by an Italian friar named Gabriele Maria Berardi."

"Okay. So what? Dalí was a showboat. He was never even possessed according to Kayo. How does this help us?" Roma didn't answer, just continued to flip through her notebook pages. Sam noticed her hands were shaking. "Roma?"

"I don't know!" she screamed. "I just want to confirm the facts. It's what I do. I just want to make sure he isn't lying to us before we decide if we can trust him."

"Roma," Sam said in the soft tone her mother would use to calm her, "he isn't lying. And this isn't going to help us. We need to figure out what we're going to do." She reached forward and gently pulled the notebook from her hands.

Roma scowled at her, but she held her tongue. With shaky fingers, she snaked a cigarette out of the pack on the coffee table and lit it. "I just need to have all the facts."

"Okay," Sam said. After a beat, she tried to lighten the mood by pointing out that residents weren't supposed to smoke in The Castle.

"Yeah, well," Roma said, "I'm not supposed to be eaten by a pagan vampire either, so…"

Taking a seat on the floor, Sam said, "We need to talk through what we know. Let's start with Imogene Kayo. She was Stanford Kayo's wife. She had tuberculosis. She died here from complications."

"No," Roma said sharply. "That's wrong. Think about how long it was inside Milo before it showed itself. It needs a strong body. And it needs to grow strong *inside* that body. I think that's what Kayo meant when he said he'd made a mistake. He summoned it to enter her because he thought it would make her strong and keep her alive. But, like he said, Imogene was too delicate to host it. She was too weak when they became entwined. And when she died, it was stuck on this property." After a pause, she asked, "I mean, don't you think? Does that sound right to you?"

Sam was taken aback by the fragility in those questions, by her need for Sam's own confirmation. "It does, yeah. Okay…so Kayo started it, we know that. It killed Imogene; we think we know that. So, Florence…?"

"I think Florence is a victim too. A 'mere innocent girl.' She's not a bad guy, Sam. No more so than Milo."

"But it's Florence who's possessing him. I've seen her. You confirmed the sketch I drew was Florence Massey."

"Florence Massey died in an asylum in Paris, remember? That's the thing that's never added up. I mean, Kayo didn't die here either, but he set all this in motion, right? This is his purgatory. Not Florence though. Kayo said the lamia was a trickster. I think it can masquerade as Florence because it used to possess her. Maybe a part of her is still inside it, I don't know. But it isn't her, not the real her. Milo let it in because it tricked him into thinking it was Florence. It probably tricked Florence too, by masquerading as Imogene."

Sam thought of the statue of Imogene Kayo standing goddess-like in her pleated robes and sandals in front of The Castle. She must have been striking to see in real life—and, possibly even more so if she appeared with the ethereal sheen of a ghost. As if it still mattered, she asked, "So, Milo isn't a murderer?"

With uncharacteristic delicacy, Roma said, "Milo was a victim, just like Florence. Just like Imogene."

A sudden rush of tears filled Sam's eyes. "Was?"

"Right, *was*. I think he's gone, Sam. I think we need to destroy them both. If we don't, then it will remain on this land. And it may even present itself as Milo the next time it tries to kill."

VII.

We had to lean a shoulder into the door of the deprivation sauna and dig the balls of our feet into the earth to start it moving. After several seconds of pushing, we felt it budge, then it began to swing open under its own weight. A weak ripple of stale air escaped the building, rolling over us and dissipating into the night. In the open doorway, we were presented with a blackness that felt as pure and vacuous as space itself. There were no lights inside, of course, not even wall mountings to hold candles or torches.

We knew our first footfall inside the building would be a downward step, that the door opened onto what was essentially the top of a long, straight staircase which led to a dirt basement. We maneuvered our load through the doorway and into the darkness, then proceeded down those stairs as if they were perfectly lit and we were in no danger of falling.

A part of us was still pondering what Stanford Kayo had told them—that Florence was an innocent girl, that the lamia wasn't Florence Massey at all.

The stronger part of us scolded these niggling thoughts.

We kept moving down the stairs to deposit our first lamb in its final place of rest. Mostly, we stayed focused on the further preparations that were needed before we could deposit the others. We had an art exhibition to arrange.

CHAPTER: 10

I.

They decided they needed a dagger. With her knowledge of the occult and her general preparedness, Sam half-expected Roma to have one—some ceremonial blade with invocations carved into its handle that she'd pull out of her backpack and say, "Oh, this? I always travel with it just in case." Instead, she looked at Sam and asked, "Do you think they have something like that in the kitchen?"

Really, they suspected anything would work—a heavy pipe or a rope or just the right number of pills. But, in movies, sacrifice rituals always used a dagger, so that's what they would use too. Roma said it was appropriate, the physical closeness of a short blade for the intimate work of taking a life. Sam hadn't responded to that. She'd only hoped Roma would be the one to do it.

As far as they knew we were still in our apartment, so they crept across the second-floor hallway with their eyes fixed on our door. When they got to the stairs, they moved down quickly, glancing back over their shoulders like we might silently appear behind them with our arms stretched in front of us like a child's idea of a monster. We didn't appear on the stairs, of course. We were finishing our work at the bottom of Kayo's depravation sauna.

The first floor was dark. Roma stepped onto the landing, and Sam kept close behind her. They passed the empty common room where board game pieces were still wildly scattered around. Sam always found it uncanny to see that communal space when it was dark and empty, but the effect was especially potent tonight. "Creepy," she muttered.

Without turning to see what she meant, Roma said, "This place is always creepy." She pulled open the dining hall door and Sam followed her through it. The taps and squeaks of their shoes echoed all around them.

"We'll probably have to settle for a chef's knife or something," Roma said. She led Sam to the kitchen entrance at the back of the dining hall. It had a single swinging door which flapped behind them after they pushed through it. Their pace had become hurried now that they were away from our apartment, so Sam nearly collided with Roma when she abruptly stopped in front of her. She was staring at something on the floor in the distance. Sam couldn't see what.

"What is it?" she asked.

Roma moved to the side and pointed. Lying on an antifatigue floor mat a few feet ahead of them was the kitchen towel we'd dropped on our way out of Fish's office. In the moonlight that shone through the kitchen window, there was no mistaking that it was spotted with blood.

"Gross," Sam said, then, after a pause, "I mean, it's animal blood, right? From one of Brandon's dinners?"

"Maybe," Roma said, unconvinced. "You check."

"What? Why me?"

"I don't know. Because I don't want to. Anyway, I dealt with your blood earlier. It's your turn."

Sam glared at her, but she couldn't argue with this logic. "What am I even checking for?" She took a tentative step past Roma, toward the kitchen towel.

"I'm not sure. Just…pick it up."

Sam looked back at her with an expression that recalled Roma's own familiar judgmental glower. She moved to the opposite side of the towel, facing Roma, then crouched for a better look. "There doesn't seem to be all that much blood, really," she said. She bent down and pinched it between her thumb and index finger. She had only lifted it a foot or so off the ground when something fell from it and hit the floor with a brief tinkling sound.

"What was that?" Roma asked.

Sam laid the towel on the metal counter beside the sink then bent down to investigate. We felt the ache in her knees as she stooped. The tiny object glimmered from a hole in the antifatigue mat. Given how sticky and oily the mat looked, she was grateful to be able to identify it without needing to pick it up. "It's just a piece of glass," she said.

"Why would there be glass in a towel he used to prepare food?"

"I…don't know," Sam said. "Maybe he broke something?"

Roma was skeptical. She came to Sam's side and stared down at the tiny shard, then looked past her into a dark corner of the kitchen. She continued in that direction, keeping her eyes on the floor in front of her. Our knuckles were still bleeding when we left the kitchen, and she followed a sporadic trail of blood splatter which had run down our fingers and dripped onto the floor tiles. She disappeared down the aisleway leading to Fish's office. Sam was just about to call after her when Roma bolted back around the corner. "He broke into the office. And, I mean, not like I did. He properly broke in. Broke the glass out of the window. I don't think that's animal blood, Sam."

Sam's face blanched, and she rose quickly, causing her injured body to scream. "He didn't—" she started. "Oh, my God! Did he get Fish too?"

"What? Oh…no, sorry. The office is empty. Milo must have cut himself when he broke in. We should check it out, though, to see if we can figure out what he was after in there."

They walked side by side, each of them privately afraid we might jump out from a shadow and attack them. When they arrived at Fish's open office door, Roma was the first to step inside. "So, he smashed through this window and cut up his hand then he cleaned it off on that towel. The question is why…"

Sam followed her into the office. The space was tight for two people. Glancing around at the clutter, she realized the room was too disorganized to tell if anything had been disturbed. She'd just noticed

Fish's laptop on the desk when Roma pointed and said, "There! That nail." Sam looked. A bent nail projected out of the wall above the desk, forming a makeshift hook. "When I was in here earlier, a ring of keys was on this nail. I remember because the ring was a big circle, and when I saw it, I thought it looked like those keyrings jailers have in old cartoons." She stared at the empty nail. "So…what do those keys open, and why does he need them?"

"They're probably just keys to the apartments, right?" Sam asked. "I mean, we know he's planning to…you know." She couldn't bring herself to say, *kill us all.*

"It's Milo." Her tone minimized us like we were some loveable pet or mascot. "If he knocked on anyone's door, they'd just let him in. Nobody knows it's not really him except for us."

"Well, maybe he wants to do it when everyone's asleep," Sam offered. She shivered at the thought.

"It's possible…"

"That must be it, right? Other than the apartments, everything in the building is open to everyone. Except for this office, and he clearly didn't need the keys for that."

"True," Roma allowed. "So maybe something outside this building, then?"

All at once, Sam arrived at the answer. "Milo mentioned something about a shed in the woods. The EMT did too. She said it was locked and the kids she knew could never force it open."

"In those paintings…" Roma began.

"The bodies were piled on a dirt floor," Sam said, completing the thought.

All at once, they heard movement echoing in the distance—the front doors opening, our footsteps. Perhaps the sound was headed toward the stairs leading up to the apartments. Perhaps not.

They gaped at one another with mirrored looks of distress. "Oh my God," Sam said, "Milo. What do we do?"

Roma listened for a moment, her eyes tilted toward the office ceiling, before she said, "He doesn't know we've learned anything. As far as he knows, we just came down for a midnight snack, or maybe we were searching for a bottle of Brandon's wine to get a little drunk or something."

"Is that our excuse if he comes in here?" Sam asked. Panic quickened her voice.

"He isn't going to come in here. He already has what he came for. And he'll assume we're asleep in our beds."

"But if he does come?"

"If he does come, we just treat him like nothing's up, everything's normal. He won't, though. He doesn't know we know." We felt how desperately she wanted this to be true, how uncertain she truly was.

They stood together, listening, shoulders touching. Sam had the impulse to grab Roma's hand and squeeze it, but she resisted. An eternity passed before they accepted that our footsteps had stopped, and they allowed themselves to believe we'd gone upstairs for now.

"What's he doing up there?" Sam asked. The question was out of her mouth before it occurred to her that the answer might be unthinkable. It might be we were letting ourselves into someone's apartment to continue the work of systematically murdering them all. Roma had already been thinking this, and her eyes were wide with alarm.

Together, they sprinted from the office back through the kitchen. Sam had just pushed through the kitchen door when, from behind her, Roma whispered, "Wait! The knife!" She turned back into the kitchen, leaving Sam alone in the dining hall.

Sam continued forward slowly and steadily, her eyes on the ceiling. Everything was quiet as far as she could tell. She heard the squeak of the kitchen door and turned to see Roma, the glint of the kitchen knife she held at her side. Sam pushed the dining hall door open and stepped out. She audibly gasped at the sight of us sitting on the stairs.

"Hey, Sam," we said. "What are you up to?"

II.

"Woah, woah. I didn't mean to scare you," we said, a goofy smile drawn across our face.

"Milo! God!" Sam leaped backward and touched her hand to her chest like she was protecting her heart from us.

"Relax, Sam," we said, rising and coming toward her. "It's just me." Twenty feet, or so, separated us. Approaching her, we were sure to slouch a little to show her everything was cool and casual.

She tried to smile, but she took a step back toward the closed dining hall doors. "I, um…I thought you were at the hospital, Milo."

"I was. Most of the night. Just got back." We shook our head and rolled our eyes like we were communicating what a hassle our hospital experience had been. When we were close enough, we reached out and touched her lightly on the arm. We registered the tiny flinch of her body. "Are you okay? Is something wrong?"

"No. Yeah, I'm fine. It's just, you scared me."

"There's nothing scary about me, Sam." We opened our arms wide in the same way Fish had on the day of our tour when he came down the stairs to meet us—*Just little old me.*

"You startled me, I meant."

"Sorry about that. I didn't mean to."

We could sense the wheels turning in her head, her desperate attempt to think of something to say that sounded natural. She settled on, "That was crazy, what happened in the common room, earlier. The seizure, or whatever? Do they know what it was?"

We shook our head like we were embarrassed with ourselves. "I don't know," we said, "They did a bunch of tests, but nothing looked off. They think it was just stress, probably. That whole big show, and it was just a panic attack. Pretty stupid, right?"

"No. I mean, panic attacks are no joke, I've heard. I'm just glad you're okay. You *are*, right, Milo? You're okay?" Despite knowing better, she longed for it to be true.

"Sam?" we asked, furrowing our brow. "Why do you keep glancing at the dining hall doors?"

Her blush was deep and immediate. "I'm not," she said with a little laugh that suggested we were silly to have asked.

"You are, though," we smiled. "You keep glancing behind you. Is there someone in there?"

"No, I just…" She paused, the wheels turning in her mind. "I feel caught, I guess. I didn't expect to see anyone, and then you appeared out of nowhere like a ghost."

"Like a ghost," we repeated as if the words were precious. "I wouldn't say I came out of nowhere exactly. But I understand what you mean." We studied the woodgrain on the dining hall doors. "So, what were you doing? Why were you sneaking around?"

"Couldn't I ask you the same thing?" She felt pleased with this response, turning our question back on us. She even stood a little straighter when she asked directly, "What are you doing sneaking around down here, Milo?"

We were amused by her attempt to play it cool. We had expected her to cower. We decided to play too, taking a step forward and cooing, "I was looking for you, Sam."

She pulled back, pressing herself into the corner beside the dining hall's entrance. We leaned in, shifting our body slightly to block any route of escape. A part of us hated it, playing like we were some toxic male asshole. Our face was near hers, and the devastation we saw there caused the slightest separation in us, similar to what had happened upstairs when we were recalling the failed ritual in 1947. Florence seemed drawn to her panic and fear as strongly as I was repelled by it. "Why were you looking for me?" Sam asked, breathless but still trying.

"Because I have a surprise for you."

Sam's irises trembled as she held her gaze on us. "I don't like surprises."

"It's a good surprise. You'll like this one, I promise."

She turned her head, listening through the door to the dining hall. "What is it?" she asked, finally.

We stepped back and held out a closed fist to her. "Here, hold out your hand."

She hesitated, but we encouraged her with a friendly smile, a little nod. Tentatively, she reached forward and opened her palm under our fist.

"Ready? Three, two, one," we said, then opened our empty hand. We held it above Sam's palm for only a second before seizing her by the wrist.

"Let go!"

Wait, I called internally to Florence. *No!* The pain that followed was beyond anything I could have imagined. It registered simultaneously in every nerve ending from the top of my head to heels of my feet—the feeling of having my physical body ripped away from any control I still had over it. I screamed and screamed, but I made no sound because my voice belonged to her now.

"Sam, dear heart," Florence said. She moved even closer to her, pinning her to the corner beside the dining hall doorway. "I missed you so. Did you miss me too?"

"No!" Sam shouted. "Milo, stop!"

"Guess again," my voice cooed.

"Florence!" she cried, "Florence, stop! Please!"

"I've been busy since I left you. I've been preparing an exhibition for you. I've made a celebration of *us.*"

I tried uselessly to pry my fingers off Sam's wrist, but it only angered Florence and made her squeeze tighter. *What are you doing?* I demanded internally.

"Florence, you need to let Milo go! Don't make him another victim. Don't do to him what it did to you." Her breathing was shallow and rapid. It felt terrible to be forced to see her so frightened.

Florence opened my throat and laughed.

I begged her to stop.

"Milo is nothing more than a lamb. My destiny is you, Sam. I only needed him to incubate, to keep you pure until I was strong enough for you. I was so weak when you arrived, and you were so frustratingly cautious. I could barely even show myself to you. But tonight, we'll dispatch him, and our spirits will become one, yours and mine. And then we will sacrifice them all."

No! I screamed inside myself. *This isn't the plan! This isn't the plan! Get out! I want you out of me! Florence!*

A voice that was raspy and unfamiliar, and which sounded only inside my head, hissed, *I am not Florence, and you will be still.* Keeping a tight hold on Sam's wrist, the thing inside me turned my body to face the tiled wall then reared back and slammed my forehead hard into it. Once, then again, and then a third time.

The assault left me stunned. I was only vaguely aware of what happened next.

Sam was cowering, watching, screaming.

Unexpectedly, the dining hall door flew open, and someone—Roma?—ran at us wielding a long, wooden rolling pin.

I instinctively tried to raise my hands in self-defense, but, of course, the thing—the lamia—wouldn't allow it. It didn't matter anyhow. Roma hadn't come for me.

Sam's screaming stopped abruptly when Roma struck her on the head with the rolling pin. Her body went limp, and she slumped to the floor, dragging out of the lamia's grip.

It screamed in my voice, and I felt a rush of pressure like my consciousness was being sucked into a vacuum. As I blacked out, I heard the evermore distant cries from Roma. Over and over, they said, "No, Florence! Take me! Take me instead!"

III.

Sam woke up with her head throbbing so violently she immediately lurched forward and threw up. For long, confused seconds, the whole world seemed to be a whirl of spinning lights and foreign sounds. She was muttering, "Mom? Mom? Mom?" in a delirious incantation.

"Shh, dear heart," a cooing voice said. Not her mom's voice. Deeper. My voice, though it wasn't me using it. We were no longer one. The lamia controlled my body completely. I had been locked away.

Sam skittered back from the sound of my voice, rising to her feet and attempting to run. The world was still spinning, though, and she staggered and fell. She tried to brace herself, but when her palms hit the ground, they slid out from under her. She grimaced, prepared for her face to slam into the ground, but she came to rest submerged up to her chest in cool water. She rose up, gasping and choking. A hand was being extended to her, and she groped for it wildly. The hand yanked her hard, and she propelled upward, onto her feet, supported by the body that had saved her.

"Milo?" she whimpered. She was pressed against my body, of course, a thought she found horrifying. Despite everything, though, she was grateful to be held.

"Not Milo, dear," my voice said tenderly. "Remember?"

Sam squinted over my shoulder and her eyes slowly brought our surroundings into focus. We were at the pond in the growing light of the new day.

"Welcome to the exhibition," the lamia said. "This is our big final show."

"I don't want to be here," Sam cried.

"But *everyone* will be here soon," it cooed. "Fish and Brandon, the twins. And your father, of course."

At the mention of Dr. Rimini, Sam attempted to struggle against the grip of my hand, but the lamia hugged her tightly and began to laugh like Sam had said something impossibly charming and adorable.

Sam screamed.

"Yes!" it said "Go on and yell out if you like. You'll only help them find us. They're waking now, anyway. We made quite a commotion preparing for our show. We've been busy little bees, Sam, since that awful girl hit you."

"Hit…?" she asked, struggling to remember.

"Oh, yes. *Hit.* With a rolling pin of all things. Right against the side of your beautiful face." It extended my finger and placed it on the bruised skin where Roma had struck her. Sam winced. The lamia made a tut-tut sound with my tongue like a mother gently scolding a naughty child. "She thought I would want her instead of you." With my hand, it tilted Sam's chin until her eyes met mine. "But how could anyone think they could compete with you, Samantha?"

Inches away from my face, staring into my familiar brown eyes, Sam felt overcome by a need to speak to me. Not the Milo Selby who was holding her against his body, but the real me who was trapped inside it. "Milo?" Her voice trembled. I tried to call out to her, but I was incapable even of that.

The lamia gave Sam a resigned grin. "I'm sorry, dear heart, Milo isn't available just now."

"Florence," Sam tried, "you have to let him go."

I felt my lips grow into a grotesque smile. "Not Florence either," my voice sang in a menacing little melody.

A tear ran down Sam's face. "I'm not talking to you!" she spat. "I'm talking to Florence. Florence, if there's any part of you inside the lamia, please help Milo get out. He was tricked, the same as you. I know this isn't your fault, but you can't let it hurt him too. You can't let it use you to hurt him the way it hurt you."

The lamia turned cold and stony as Sam spoke. In a flat tone, it said, "I parted ways with Florence ages ago. I kept something of her, though, as a souvenir of our time together—her memories, her talents. She went mad without them. As for Milo…he's done some things he isn't proud of. If he survives the transition when we fuse, we could keep him alive, I suppose, to answer for his brother…and for all the other mess we'll leave behind us tonight. Would that make your heart feel lighter? To leave him for the authorities to find, ranting about ghosts and covered in so much of your friends' blood?"

Sam hung her head.

"No, I didn't think so. Well, then…should we get on with our exhibition?" The lamia stepped back from Sam and gingerly released her, so she was standing under her own power. "We've already set everything up." It extended my hand and turned my body like some circus ringleader presenting her with the greatest show on earth.

Sam peered into the distance, at the landscape surrounding the pond. The sun hadn't yet risen over the tree line. At first, she saw only variants of darkness, shadows of deeper or lesser intensity. As her eyes focused, though, she began to make out figures standing all around the pond's muddy bank. Her first thought was ghosts—spirits of the property's old artists, maybe, or of that earlier generation of elites who were mistreated by Stanford Kayo. Quickly, though, she realized she was wrong. Those human-like figures weren't human at all. They were makeshift easels—tall crosses made of tree limbs onto which our grotesque paintings had been nailed or tied. In some cases, two or more canvases of different sizes were displayed together in an overlapping arrangement. One easel for every resident.

"I've already seen these," Sam said, like it would make any difference.

"No, dear, you *viewed* them, unartfully scattered on a floor. It's only in their proper context that you can truly *see* them."

"I won't help you do what's in those portraits."

The lamia tossed my hand. "Well," it said, "if you won't, you won't." It walked a few yards away from her, into the darkness, then bent to retrieve something from the grass. When it returned, it was holding a crude torch made from a tree limb with a torn shirt wrapped around the far end. Sam recognized the smell of the turpentine that dripped from the fabric. She registered a brief, indistinguishable movement of my other arm, then a flicking sound, before the fabric burst into flame with an audible *whoosh*.

Sam gazed at my face, lit from below, dark shadows rising upward as if they were trying to slide up my skin and into the night sky. "A gift from that awful girl," the lamia said, showing Sam what she could now see was Roma's cheap plastic cigarette lighter.

The lamia walked by Sam so close she could feel the heat of its torch. "The thing I liked about Milo," it called as it continued into the distance, "is that he was in so much pain, pain which is infinitely deeper than yours. He can paint too, of course. Not as well as you and I might have painted together. Nowhere near that well. But he was hurt, and that hurt made him…easier. More accepting. He was a safer space than you. While I was weak, a safe space was what I needed." The lamia stopped in front of a wooden cross and lifted the torch to examine the paintings affixed to it.

Even from a distance, Sam could see they fit together to form the sickening likeness of Jack.

The lamia turned to Sam and motioned at the collage with its torch. "In time, Milo might well have done this to Jack even without me. Not in this way, of course, but he was so fearful of Big Brother, and fear can so easily turn to hate." It took a final, appraising look into Jack's dead, painted eyes before touching the torch to the canvases. They were instantly consumed by fire. The lamia held out my arms, lifted my face to the sky, and screamed with primal pleasure. The sound caused a rattling in the treetops like it had awoken the very terrain surrounding us.

Sam became aware of a distant whimpering. In the rapidly waning firelight from the canvas, she perceived a form crouched against another of the makeshift crosses. She squinted and took a few unsteady steps toward it. "Roma?"

"Yes, yes, Roma," the lamia said dismissively. It pushed the torch in Roma's direction but was far enough away that no light was cast onto her.

"Sam," Roma said weakly. "Sam, help me. Help me, I can't move."

The lamia walked steadily toward her. Sam followed at a distance. "And why would she help you?" it asked. "Sam, come closer so Roma can see that terrible knot on your temple. Let her look at her handywork."

Having found Sam in the darkness, Roma pleaded with her, "Sam, don't listen to him. I didn't mean it. I never meant to hurt you."

The lamia's laugh rang out in pulsing waves which echoed into the distance. "No, of course she didn't mean to hurt you. She was merely showing her affection for you. With a rolling pin to the temple."

"No," Roma whimpered.

"Yes," Sam said. She came closer, careful to keep at a distance from the lamia. "You did though. You attacked me. What the hell?" Now that she was close, Sam could see Roma was tied up with what appeared to be torn kitchen towels. Above her was her own painted likeness, throat slit, in a horrible state of death. Her cheeks, wet from crying, reflected smudges of torchlight.

"No! I was trying to save you!" Roma pleaded. "I was trying to keep it from taking you."

"Such a selfless girl," The lamia sneered. "Does that characterization track with what we know about our little Roma? *Selflessness?* I hardly think so."

"Stop it!" Roma screamed.

"Let's give it some thought—Roma shows up out of nowhere to treat you like, what? An insect? A bug? She makes you feel like you're not pretty enough. Not cool enough. Not smart enough."

"Don't listen to her, Sam. It got in my head in the dining hall. It made me think I had to hit you to save you."

"And how is it that our Roma has always been so very knowledgeable? Strange, isn't it, that she could always find the answers you needed? That she'd dug so far into the history of this property? Into ghosts and ghoulies? Into conjuring the dead?"

"Sam…"

"It's almost as if she already knew. It's almost as if she was stringing you along."

"I wasn't! I honestly wasn't!"

"As if she knew it was *you* whom I was preparing for, *you* whom I wanted to give everything to. An exceptional life this sarcastic little girl could only dream of."

"Shut up! Please…" Roma sobbed.

"And she kept you close so she could steal what was rightfully yours. As if she could ever be mistaken for divine."

"*Shut up!*" This time she screamed the words, causing that elemental force to rustle again in the trees.

Without realizing it, Sam had allowed the lamia to close the distance between them. It was pacing back and forth in a half-circle behind the cross that held Roma's portrait. Sam was standing farther back, but still close enough that it could rush and grab her.

"She manipulated you, Sam, from the very start. Flirting and withholding. Blatantly smoking in front of you to remind you of your mother, dead from lung cancer. Her occasional, motherly treatment of you."

This point caused a pit to form in Sam's stomach. She couldn't be sure about anything else it was saying, but it was true that thoughts of her mother flashed through her mind every time she smelled Roma's cigarette smoke.

"No, Sam. I never did any of that. I didn't even know your mom smoked. You never told me."

The lamia stopped pacing. "You couldn't tell it upset her?" It clucked my tongue. "Lies make souls turn black as ash, little girl."

"No!" Roma wailed, shaking the trees. "I'm not lying! I didn't mean to do that! I know I'm not nice sometimes, but it isn't what he's saying. It isn't like that."

In the distance beyond the tree line, a voice called out in response to Roma's cries: "Sam?"

It was Dr. Rimini.

The seconds that followed were a chaos of Roma's bloody screams for help and the responses from the others, yelling for her and for Sam and for me, of the treetops talking in rustles and squawks. In those seconds of distraction, the lamia flung the torch in Roma's direction. Sam's eyes instinctively followed its light. She gasped when the canvases with Roma's death mask caught fire only inches above her bound body.

While she was distracted by the growing flames and their danger to Roma, a great scream emitted from my mouth as the lamia pushed out of me and lunged at Sam. It struck her with a force so powerful it knocked her onto her back in the grass beside the pond.

My own spent body slumped to the ground. My awareness floated outside of me, separated from that used-up body, homeless.

The lamia was now a pressure on Sam's face and chest. It felt to her like it was trying to force itself into her through each of the tiny pores in her skin. She resisted, pushing out with everything inside her, imagining a field of energy between the lamia's will and her own, like two opposing magnets being squeezed together.

In the distance, Roma's pleas became cries of terror as the fire burned above her head, hot embers drifting down into her hair and onto her neck and shoulders. The rustling in the trees drew closer as if the elemental force was swooping down around us for a better view of the mounting chaos. Sam was aware of the voices of the others, nearer now.

The lamia pressed harder into her. It wasn't visible as an apparition, but it had grown so strong inside me that Sam could make out its features bending the air above her—the curl of its hideous lips as it pushed closer, the slither of its serpent-like tail. Sam, herself, began to weaken, and she closed her eyes to it, a tear falling down her cheek as she accepted that the fight was draining out of her. All at once, her will collapsed. Just when she expected to feel her body overtaken, a loud, angry sound screamed in her ear. The feeling of something sharp and serrated like a kitchen knife sliced across her cheek, followed by a rush of air across her body. The pressure of the lamia pushing into her was suddenly gone, swallowed by whatever had forced itself between them.

Sam skittered backward, away from where it attacked her. Dr. Rimini was running toward her, but he slowed as his attention was taken by something above his head.

Sam followed his eyes. The sky above the pond was churning with the silhouettes of broad-winged birds—hundreds of great blue herons flying in a circular formation. At the center of that circle was a single bird in upward flight. It was this same heron which had forced itself between Sam and the lamia, taking the demon into its own body, sacrificing itself, and now it was rising on its strong wings, growing smaller and smaller. Soon, Sam lost sight of it in the half-light of the early morning sky.

Dr. Rimini's arms were around her now. He was kneeling, calling her name, but Sam's attention remained on the flock of birds, at the empty sky at the center of the circle they'd formed. Seconds passed, and suddenly that single heron reappeared—first as a speck, then as a defined shape. She wrestled one arm out of her dad's embrace and pointed, drawing his attention to it. The great blue heron descended rapidly like a projectile, like a crashing plane, not spinning as if it were lifeless and falling from the sky, but streamlined, its long, graceful neck pointed straight down, directing it toward some target below. In another second, its agonized squawking became so loud it was almost too heartbreaking for her to bear. "No," Sam muttered, turning away as it broke the surface of the pond with a mighty splash which felt as violent as the mouth of the underworld being forced open to reclaim a demon into whatever Hell lay beyond it.

In the distance, Fish managed to untie Roma from her burning cross.

Brandon held the twins with their faces pressed into his thighs, shielding them.

Dr. Rimini held Sam as she cried something over and over about her mother saving her.

I became aware that I was staring up at the sky with my actual eyes, returned to my body, watching each of those many birds turn to silhouettes against the rising sun until the last of them disappeared.

CHAPTER: 11

The problem with horror movies is they never really show you what happens after the monster's slayed. I mean, there might be a scene where the final girl waits at the bus stop, or whatever, the morning after she defeated the evil stalking her town, but that's not what I'm talking about. Those scenes are only meant to signify the end of the movie, that life is back to normal and all is well. Roll credits. Exit through the lobby.

What I mean is those movies never look back at the impact of the horrors they show us. They skip the funerals of all the people whose deaths we forgot about because they were only minor characters. They weren't the star, so we don't care. But if they'd show those funerals— attended by row after row of heartbroken extras who only enter the film in those scenes—we'd realize every single one of them was a star to somebody. They were loved, and they matter. The filmmakers don't want us to think about that.

And, as for the final girls, you don't just get on the school bus the morning after your friends have been killed, and you were forced to do terrible things to save yourself from that same fate. It's misleading. Suggesting they repress those experiences and get on with life is as horrifying as the evils depicted in those movies. In real life, every single one of them would be forever screwed up because they were expected to keep their chins up and push their feelings down. It would be too much for anyone. The way those movies end is dangerous. They give people the wrong idea. Talking through your feelings is important. I've learned that since I've been here. This place has been good for me.

The Indiana district attorney fought hard against it. He tried me as an adult for Jack's murder and was hoping to put me away for life in a maximum-security prison. Our side pleaded insanity, though, and somehow, we won. I'm still working through how I feel about claiming in a court of law that it was all in my head, but my counsel told me it was a one-in-a-million decision. Apparently, insanity defenses almost never work. At any rate, I'm getting help here. I think it's the kind of help I would have needed even if we'd never moved to The Castle, even if Jack were still alive and out there somewhere, embarrassed his kid brother was locked up in a loony bin.

We talk a lot about Jack. Of course, we do. He died by my hand, even if I wasn't the one to kill him.

The lamia said I still might have hurt him even if it never got inside me. I used to believe it, but not anymore. I've learned some things about trauma since I've been here. I've come to understand just how much of it we were both carrying around and not dealing with, how it shaped our whole relationship after Mom and Dad died. I didn't hate Jack. Maybe he hated me, I don't know; he certainly acted like he did. Honestly, though, I'm skeptical. I think we were two people whose worlds were pulled out from under us, and we were too damaged to know how to rebuild together. We might have figured it out eventually, but I can't know for sure. That's something I'll need to learn to live with. I would never hurt him, though, not if I could help it. I'm certain about that.

I mentioned horror movies because they come up a lot in sessions with my therapists. Whether they believe me about Florence Massey and the lamia, they all seem to accept that horror tropes are the easiest way available for us to talk about what happened, and talking about your feelings is the most important thing.

For all I know, they might believe me. After all, it was big news. It became a national story. I was already a monster in the eyes of the local news anchors in Muncie because of Rebecca Steiner. They were all too willing to grab the national spotlight by telling the world how they'd seen me coming for months, how I'd been a ticking time bomb. They're wrong, but I don't blame them.

I'm not certain this is the appropriate place, but I'm going to say it anyway—I feel terrible about Rebecca. My therapists and I discuss her too, and while I feel confident to say her death wasn't my fault, it's also true that my actions were inappropriate and unacceptable. Sure, I couldn't have known what was going on in her life, but that's kind of the point. You never know what struggles someone is going through, so you can't know what effect it will have when you flip them the bird or call them a name or say something mean about them online. I'm not responsible for her death, but I'm responsible for my actions, and my actions were harmful. The same with Jack, in a way.

I got a letter from Dr. Rimini a few days ago. It's the only correspondence I've received from anyone I actually know. He said Roma packed up and disappeared that night, gone back home to work things out with her mother, he assumes. Fish and Brandon gave Dr. Rimini thirty days' notice that they were closing the community, but he got Sam out of there long before then. Sam's doing well, he says, but there are some things she doesn't remember. She's never wavered from her story that I was possessed by an evil spirit, though, that it was the lamia, and not me, who did those terrible things. The fact that he mentioned it suggests he believes her, I guess. Still, I can't help but wonder why she's never written to me herself.

After receiving his letter, I decided to write all this down. Partly, I wanted to help Sam fill in the pieces she's blocked out. But there are also parts of this story she's never known, things only I can tell her. I think I'm the only person in the world, for example, who knows the life story of Florence Massey. Not the evil force that impersonated her, but the actual, extraordinary woman who's otherwise been lost to history.

The hospital offers a journaling course, and they tell us that when you write you should always envision your perfect reader. Sam, you're my perfect reader. I wrote this for you. If you ever see it, I hope it helps you. If you make it this far, I want you to know I'm sorry. Some of what I did was outside my control, but it only got that far because I tried to deceive you. The lamia was a monster, but it was right about every good thing it said about you. It was correct about the potential it saw in you. Whether you ever see this, I hope you know not to pretend you're okay when you're not. And to ask for help when you need it. If you see this, I hope it's helpful to you. Even if it only helps you put this in the past. I hope, with all my heart, that your future is unburdened.

Your friend, Milo Selby

ABOUT THE AUTHOR

M.C. Schmidt's fiction has appeared in numerous literary journals and anthologies, including Southern Humanities Review, EVENT, The Saturday Evening Post, and Coolest American Stories 2024. He has an MFA in creative writing and lives in Ohio where he walks six miles a day. When not reading or listening to music, he can be found baking with his best friend, a sourdough starter named Bronwyn.

NOTE FROM M.C. SCHMIDT

Word-of-mouth is crucial for any author to succeed. If you enjoyed *Mad as Birds*, please leave a review online—anywhere you are able. Even if it's just a sentence or two. It would make all the difference and would be very much appreciated.

Thanks!
M.C. Schmidt

We hope you enjoyed reading this title from:

BLACK ROSE writing™

www.blackrosewriting.com

Subscribe to our mailing list – *The Rosevine* – and receive **FREE** books, daily deals, and stay current with news about upcoming releases and our hottest authors.
Scan the QR code below to sign up.

Already a subscriber? Please accept a sincere thank you for being a fan of Black Rose Writing authors.

View other Black Rose Writing titles at www.blackrosewriting.com/books and use promo code **PRINT** to receive a **20% discount** when purchasing.